About Nina Harrington

Nina grew up in rural Northumberland, England, and decided at the age of eleven that she was going to be a librarian—because then she could read *all* of the books in the public library whenever she wanted! Since then she has been a shop assistant, community pharmacist, technical writer, university lecturer, volcano walker and industrial scientist, before taking a career break to realise her dream of being a fiction writer. When she is not creating stories which make her readers smile her hobbies are cooking, eating, enjoying good wine—and talking, for which she has had specialist training.

™

GIRLS JUST WANT TO HAVE FUN

Girls, gossip and gorgeous guys

Fabulous Riva™ author Nina Harrington
brings you a brand-new trilogy, exploring the lives
and loves of best friends Amber, Kate and Saskia.

Life might have taken them from exotic India
to exclusive London and the exquisite French Alps,
but when their heads are in a spin over a gorgeous guy
they are always there for each other.

Don't miss
The First Crush Is the Deepest
June 2013

Last-Minute Bridesmaid
August 2013

and

Blame It on the Champagne
October 2013

Blame It on the Champagne

Nina Harrington

MILLS & BOON

First published in Great Britain 2013
by Mills & Boon, an imprint of Harlequin (UK) Limited.
Harlequin (UK) Limited, Eton House, 18-24 Paradise Road,
Richmond, Surrey TW9 1SR

© Nina Harrington 2013

ISBN: 978 0 263 23568 5

Harlequin (UK) policy is to use papers that are natural, renewable
and recyclable products and made from wood grown in sustainable
forests. The logging and manufacturing process conform to the
legal environmental regulations of the country of origin.

Printed and bound in Great Britain
by CPI Antony Rowe, Chippenham, Wiltshire

Also by Nina Harrington

Did you know these are also available as eBooks?
Visit www.millsandboon.co.uk

CHAPTER ONE

Elwood House: Must-Do list—Monday
- *Meet up with Kate and Amber to finalise Amber's wedding—do NOT let Kate talk you into fuchsia or satin—walk away from the satin.*
- *Decide on classical music pieces for the bathrooms.*
- *Be ready to fend off that very persistent new wine merchant.*
- *Stay in for the garden centre delivery of the spiral box trees for the front porch.*

'Snow. I am going to need lots of snow. And tiny white fairy lights sparkling in the trees and over the pergola. Can you do fairy lights?' Amber's voice tailed off into a dreamy whisper. 'It would be so magical and romantic.'

Saskia Elwood rolled her eyes and grinned at her best friend Amber, then clicked in the box next to the garden lighting option on her wedding planner spreadsheet.

'Of course I can do white fairy lights. As for the snow? That shouldn't be too difficult for New Year's Day in London. But, you know me, if you want it to snow on your wedding day, then snow you shall have, even if I have to track down a snow gun machine and make you some. Although... Won't it be a bit cold? From the designs I have seen, that dress Kate is making for you would be perfect for a tropical beach wedding—but London in January? Brr...'

Amber giggled and flicked her long straight blonde hair over one shoulder in a move she had perfected in fashion shoots and as years performing as a concert pianist. 'I know,' she replied, wrinkling up her nose in delight. 'It is so perfect. Sam is going to love it.' Then she sighed out loud and strolled out past Saskia and through the conservatory into the garden with a faraway expression on her face. 'Just love it.'

'She's off again,' a cheery voice sounded from behind Saskia's shoulder as Kate Lovat bounced into the room with a bundle of wedding magazines in her arms. 'Dreaming of the fabulous Sam. If I wasn't so smitten with my Heath I would find it a bit sickening. In fact, sometimes I'm surprised you put up with the two of us. Always talking about the lucky men who we have agreed to marry one day.'

'Right now,' Saskia replied with a snort, 'I am more worried about Amber getting frostbite in that skimpy, mostly backless dress you are planning for a winter wedding. Any chance of a jacket? Thermal vest? The poor girl is going to be blue, which is not a good look for any bride.'

Kate replied by playfully hitting Saskia on the head with a rolled up bridal magazine and sat down next to her at the conservatory table. 'Blue? With that fabulous suntan? No chance.' Then she relaxed and rested her elbows on the table. 'Relax. There is a beautiful full-length quilted ivory coat to go on top of that slinky dress for any outdoor photos. Fear not. The girl shall not freeze. When the dancing starts she will be glad of that layered silk gown, even if the beads will be flying everywhere.'

Kate arched her eyebrows and peered at Saskia's computer screen, her green eyes bright with amusement. 'Does that say dinner and reception for twenty-six? I thought this was just going to be a small family wedding. As in no professional musicians, fashion models or anybody else in Amber's world who will make us feel totally inadequate as human beings.'

Saskia laughed out loud and started counting out on her fingers. 'How could you forget Amber's first dad and his huge new stepfamily, her second dad Charles Sheridan—' she pointed towards Kate, who waved a magazine in the air '—with Heath and his new family. Her third dad might bring his new wife but she is having some "freshening up" surgery post-Christmas and might not have the stitches out in time. Oh, and her mum, of course. Julia is bringing the latest beau plus entourage, including her aunt and three American cousins and...' the air whooshed out of Saskia's lungs '...twenty-six hungry, cold people are going to celebrate the best wedding they have ever been to. Amber's friend Parvita and her husband are looking after the music and I booked the waiting staff last week. All I have to do is enjoy myself.'

'Um. Yeah. Right,' Kate replied and looked over the top of her spectacles at her. 'And exhaust yourself in the process of getting everything ready up front so it looks easy on the day. Who is kidding who here? We know you far too well, girl.' Kate smiled and gave her a one-armed hug. 'Now, let me see that list again. Aha. Thought so. You have missed out a crucial item. Tut tut.'

'What?' Saskia glanced at the screen in disbelief and then back to Kate. 'I spent most of my Sunday double-checking the plan. Out with it. What have I missed?'

Kate slid out of her chair and came around to stand in front of Saskia. 'Wedding date for a very picky hostess to be provided by her pals. Tall, dark and handsome. Dancing skills an advantage but will settle for extra hot. And you're not typing that in.'

Saskia sat back in her chair and lifted both hands into the air. 'Trust you to find me a date? Oh no. I still remember that graphic designer who offered to paint my portrait if I stripped down to earrings and a cheeky grin.'

Kate fluttered her eyelashes and tugged down the hem of her perfectly fitted jacket over her petite curves. 'We do such good work.'

Saskia snorted and turned back to the laptop. 'Thank you for the offer but the last thing I want is a boyfriend. You do know that this is the first wedding that Elwood House has ever seen, so no pressure at all.'

Kate waved her arms around and then cocked her head on one side and pushed out her lips. 'This house is gorgeous and that curvy staircase was made for a bride to walk down on her father's arm. *It is going to be fabulous,* even if we do feel guilty about leaving you to do most of the work.'

Saskia took a breath then shrugged off the lingering disquiet by tapping her wristwatch with her home-manicured fingertip.

'And I feel bad that I am making you late for your sexy lingerie fitting appointment. You know, the one that you booked three weeks ago.' She waggled her fingertips at Kate. 'Go. A new wine merchant and his sales team will be here soon and the last thing they want to see are you two drooling over wedding brochures. Scoot. And have a great time!'

Kate gasped, whooped, flung the magazines onto the table and ran out to grab hold of Amber's arm. Two minutes later all that was left of Amber and Kate were empty coffee cups and plates, a whiff of couture perfume, lipstick on her cheek and a smile on Saskia's face that only spending breakfast with her two best friends in the world could bring.

They had known each other since high school. Totally different in every way and yet she could not want better pals. They might only have reconnected at a high school reunion that May, but now it felt as though they had never been apart.

Had it only been May? Wow. So much had happened in the past few months. Amber was engaged to Sam and spending most of her time living the dream in India, while Kate was sharing her home with Amber's stepbrother Heath only a few streets away. They were both so happy... and off to be fitted with sexy lingerie by the most famous bra shop in London.

Suddenly the wedding planning spreadsheet lost its appeal and Saskia sniffed and sat back in her chair. She envied them the luxury of having time to spend comparing fine lingerie, while she was sitting here trying to decide on whether to have background music in the bathrooms. Or not.

Ah. The joys of running your home as a private meeting venue.

A whisper of self-pity flitted into her mind but she instantly pushed it to the back of her brain in disgust.

She had so much to be grateful for. Her friends Kate and Amber were the perfect pretend family who knew her a lot better than her absent parents. And then she had her home, Elwood House the architectural masterpiece which she had shared with her Aunt Margot until last year.

A gentle breeze wafted in from the garden outside the conservatory room and Saskia smiled out at the hardwood planters overflowing with autumn blossoms.

She had spent so many summer evenings with her aunt in this very room, talking and talking about their grand plan to transform Elwood House into a fabulous private dining venue. Her aunt had been the acclaimed wine expert with superb taste in interior design who was happy to leave Saskia to work on the details and business plans. Together they had been a genius team who had started the project together.

It was so sad that her aunt had never seen those plans come to fruition.

Shuffling to her feet, Saskia gathered up the breakfast dishes and loaded the dishwasher. Clasping hold of the marble worktop, she let her arms take the weight and closed her eyes for a second and took a couple of breaths.

The past six months had been harder than she had expected.

A lot harder and much more expensive. But she could not think like that. She had to make her home into a successful business because the alternative was too terrible to think about. A day job in the city would not come close to meeting the running expenses of a house this size.

Elwood House had been the home of the most famous wine merchants in London for over one hundred and fifty years. It was strange to think that she was the last in the line and responsible for preserving the heritage of the house the first of the Elwood clan had built in this smart part of London.

It was her safety net. Her home. Her sanctuary. And her security.

Saskia inhaled deeply and waggled her shoulders to release the tension.

No matter what it took or how many hours she had to work, Elwood House was going to pay for itself.

Patience. That was what she needed. Patience and a lot of new bookings.

She had only been going a few months and it took time

to get a private meeting venue like hers off the ground. Reputation spread by word of mouth and she was already attracting repeat clients, but it was a mightily slow process and she had a big gap to fill before the Christmas party season started. Maybe Amber's wedding would turn things around and she could start the New Year with hope and excitement burning in her heart?

And as for a date for Amber's wedding? That was so not going to happen. She had served meals and coffee to an awful lot of businessmen over the past few months but she had not the slightest interest in dating any of them. Just the opposite. She had learnt the hard way the cost of giving up your independence and she had no intention of repeating her mother's mistake any time soon.

Her gaze fell onto one of the wedding magazines that Kate had brought for Amber to look at and a headline on the cover leapt out at her.

Read all about the huge rise in Civil weddings at home. Celebrate your wedding in the intimate and private venue of your own home.

A spark of an idea flashed bright. *Civil weddings.* Now that was a thought. Amber's wedding might be the first wedding reception that Elwood House had seen. But it need not be the last... Um... Perhaps there was a market for small private house weddings in a city this size. Not everyone wanted an extravaganza of a huge hotel banqueting suite.

The idea was still rattling around inside her head a few minutes later when the telephone rang. Saskia barely had a chance to pick up the handset and say the words 'Elwood House,' before a transatlantic female voice belted out down the line at such a rapid-fire pace that she had to hold the phone away from her ear for a second.

'Oh, good morning, Angela. Yes, I am still available

to talk to Mr Burgess and his team today. Not a problem at all. And there has been a change to the agenda. Right. Have you got the details? Tell me everything.'

Rick Burgess leant his elbows on the solid white railings of Waterloo Bridge and watched the water taxis mooring at the jetty below. The River Thames flowed beneath his feet and wound in wide lazy curves eastwards towards the sea. Stretched out across the horizon in front of him, high-rise marvels of modern architecture reached tall into the sky against the backdrop of landmark ancient cathedrals and majestic stone buildings that made up the city of London.

A fresh breeze wafted up the river and Rick inhaled deeply, his chest rising under his white open-necked shirt and soft black leather biker jacket.

Fresh air.

Just what he needed to clear his head after being cooped up inside an aircraft and then underground trains for the past four hours.

He ran his fingers back through his tousled dark brown hair.

Yesterday he had spent the afternoon talking wine over a plate of antipasti in a sunlit garden on a Tuscan estate with a young Italian couple who had sold everything they had to buy a tiny prestigious vineyard that he knew would be taking the world by storm in time. And today he was in London under a cloudy sky with only patches of blue peeking through to lighten the grey stone buildings.

He knew exactly where he preferred to be and it certainly was not here!

It was on mornings like this that it hit more powerfully than ever that it should be his older brother Tom who should be getting ready to go into a crucial sales meeting with one of the most prestigious private dining venues in London. *Not him.*

Tom had been the businessman. The IT genius who had transformed a small chain of family wine shops into Burgess Wine, the largest online wine merchant on the West Coast of America.

Rick shook his head and chuckled. He had a pretty good idea of what Tom would've said about the crazy enterprise he was just about to launch in this city and the language would not be fit for his parents to hear.

Tom had been a conservative businessman to the core. He would never have taken a risk with a group of independent young winemakers making tiny amounts of wine on family estates across Europe.

Not all of the wine was remarkable yet. But some of it was amazing.

It was going to have to be if he had any chance at all of redeeming himself in the eyes of the media. As far as the wine trade press were concerned, Rick had certainly never earned his place on the board of directors of Burgess Wine. *Far from it.*

To them, Rick Burgess would always be every bit the renegade who had walked away from a job with the family wine business to become a professional extreme sports personality. What did he know about the modern wine trade?

And they were right.

If Tom was still alive his business ambitions would have stayed in the world he knew—professional sports and adventure tourism. They had always been his passion and still were.

But Tom was dead. And there was nothing he could do to bring him back.

Just like he couldn't change that fact that his parents

were both in their sixties and needed him to take Tom's place and work for Burgess Wine.

It had never been his decision or his choice. But as they said, there was nobody else. Burgess Wine was a family business and he had just been promoted to the son and heir whether he wanted the job or not.

Mostly not.

He didn't like it. They didn't like it. And they still didn't completely trust him not to mess things up or run back to his old life.

Emotional blackmail only went so far.

This was probably why they'd set up this sales meeting with an important client he had never met. Of course they would deny it if he questioned them, but he had been long enough in the sports world to recognise a challenge when he was presented with one.

This sales pitch was just one more way they were asking him to prove that he could pull off his crazy idea to open a flagship wine store for Burgess Wine in London.

Which in his book was even more of a reason why he had to make the wine world take him seriously. *And fast.* Even if he did detest every second of these types of business meetings.

The upbeat rhythm of a popular dance track sang out from the breast pocket of his jacket and Rick flipped open his smartphone.

'Finally! Were you actually planning to check your emails some time this morning, Rick?'

'Angie, sweetheart.' Rick chuckled. 'How delightful to hear your welcoming voice. I have just got off the plane and getting used to being back in London. Turns out I miss my chalet in France almost as much as I miss you.'

'Sweet talker! Sometimes I don't know why I put up with you. Oh. I remember now—you pay me to sort out the boring stuff in your life. But forget sightseeing for the moment—I'll take you on a tour later. Right now I need you to take your head out of the latest extreme sports magazine and flip over to the message which I am sending… now. I have some news about the sales meeting this morning, but don't worry, it's all under control.'

Rick straightened his back and turned away from the river, suddenly very wide awake.

'Good news or bad news? Talk to me, Angie. I thought we locked down this meeting weeks ago.'

His personal assistant knew him well enough to immediately gush out, 'We did. But do you remember those two TV wine experts who we approached to help promote the new store in the build-up to the launch? The ones who were so terribly busy appearing on cookery shows to get involved with yet another wine merchant? Well, guess who emailed me late last night. Apparently they heard a rumour that Elwood House might be investing in the new generation wines and suddenly they might be interested after all.'

Angie laughed down the cellphone. 'Turns out your mother was right. The Elwood Brothers connection has paid off.'

Rick exhaled slowly, pushed back his stiff shoulders and flicked through the research information on the people he was going to have to convince to take him seriously.

'Got it. I should be there in about ten minutes. And thanks for sorting out things at the London end, Angie.'

'No problem. We have an hour before the presentation. Catch up with you soon.'

Rick closed down the phone and stared at it for a few seconds before popping back into his pocket with a snort.

So that was how the game was played.

The top wine experts he needed were only prepared to turn up and listen to what he had to say if he had the credibility of a famous name in the wine trade like Elwood Brothers behind him.

Yet another example of exactly the kind of old world narrow-minded network he detested. Instead of asking what he could bring to the business, all they were looking for was the validation of the old and worthy established family of wine merchants.

Rick exhaled slowly.

Was this how it was going to be from now on?

This was not his life! His life was base jumping and pushing his body to the limit under blue skies and cold air. Not walking into a conference room and selling the idea for Rick Burgess Wines to closed minded traditional hotel owners who had already made up their minds before they heard that he said.

He was about to take the biggest leap in his life and launch a flagship wine store in the centre of London. His name above the door. His future on the line.

Only this time it was not about him or his reputation as a daredevil sportsman. This time it was about passion. A passion for life, a passion for wine, and a new passion for championing small businesses.

Rick Burgess the mountaineer. Rick Burgess the champion paraglider. And now Rick Burgess the wine merchant. Same passion. Same determination to prove that he was up to the challenge he had set himself, even if it had been foisted onto him.

Frustration burned through his veins.

He inhaled slowly, pushed off from the railing and strode away over the bridge.

He needed this to work for the employees and winemakers who relied on him and for his parents who were still locked inside their grief.

He had the presentation in his head. He had time to

spare to calm down and clear his head before facing one of the greatest challenges in his life. Bring it on.

Ten minutes later Rick turned the corner towards the address that Angie had given him, his hands in the trouser pockets of his designer denims and the breeze at his back.

A flock of pigeons swooped down in front of him into the tall oak and London plane trees which filled the small residential square. Families and dog walkers flittered between ornamental flower beds and wooden benches in the broken sunshine. On the face of it, just another quiet city square.

But one thing was certain, in the crazy world that was his life—you never knew what to expect.

Like now, for example.

It wasn't every day that you saw an executive secretary having a row with a delivery driver in the middle of a prestigious London street, but it certainly made a change from dodging tiny dogs on glittery leads. Even if the pretty girls on the other end of those leads had been trying to catch his eye.

Rick slowed his steps.

He needed to take some time out before facing an incredulous wine buyer around a conference table in some soulless, stuffy meeting room. Or the first person to mention the words 'dead man's shoes' would end up being decked, which would be a seriously bad move in more ways than one.

This was a far more entertaining option.

His girl was standing with her pretty hands splayed out on both hips and she was definitely a secretary but an executive one.

She was wearing a slim-fitting skirt suit in that strange shade of grey which his mother liked, but had never clinched a tiny waist with a cream coloured sash. He could just make out the tiny band of cream fabric at the cuffs of the jacket. Her long, sleek sandy coloured hair was gathered into a low ponytail at the nape of her neck.

Her very lovely long, smooth neck.

Now that was a neck he could look at all day.

As he watched, the shorter older man in the overalls who she was talking to in a low, patient, but very assertive voice, which reminded him of his junior school headmistress, suddenly shrugged, gave her a 'nothing to do with me' flick of both hands, jumped into a white delivery van and drove off, leaving the city girl standing on the pavement, watching the tail lights of the van disappear around the corner.

She stood frozen to the spot for a few seconds, her mouth slightly open, and then turned to glare at a pair of large shiny navy blue ceramic pots which were standing next to her on the pavement.

A five feet tall cone of what looked to Rick like a green cypress tree spilled out over the top of each planter then whirled upwards in some deformed mutant spiral shape which had nothing to do with nature and everything to do with so-called style.

Rick looked at the two plants and then back to the girl, who had started to pace up and down the pavement in platform high heeled slingback shoes, which most of the girls at his mother's office back in California seemed to wear.

Not exactly the best footwear for moving heavy pots.

But they certainly did the trick when it came the highlighting a pair of gorgeous legs with shapely ankles.

So what if he was a leg man and proud? And she had brightened up his morning.

He could make time for some excellent distraction activity.

'Good morning,' he said in a bright casual voice. 'Do you need some help with those?'

Her feet kept walking up and down. 'Do you have a trolley handy?'

He patted his pockets. 'I'm afraid not.'

'Then thank you but no.' She nodded, then stopped and stared at the huge plants, with the fingers of one hand pressed against her forehead as though she was trying to come up with a solution.

'Good thing it's not raining.' He smiled. 'In fact it is turning out to be a lovely September morning.'

Her head slowly turned towards him and Rick was punched straight in the jaw by a pair of the most stunning pale blue eyes that he had ever seen. The colour of the sky over Mont Blanc at dawn. Wild cornflowers in an alpine meadow.

Dark eyelashes clashed against the creamy clear complexion and high elegant cheekbones. Full-blown lips were outlined in a delicious shade of blush lipstick, and as she gawped at him a faint white smile caught him by surprise.

'Yes, I suppose it is.' She blinked. 'But, if you'll excuse me, I really do need to find some way of moving these plants—' she flung the flat edge of her hand towards the nearest plant and almost knocked it flying '—from the pavement into my porch and some time in the next ten minutes would be good.'

'The delivery driver?' he asked casually.

She sniffed and closed her eyes, teeth gritted tight together, then lifted her chin and smiled. 'Bad back. Not part of his job description. Just delivery to the kerbside.' Her voice lifted into a slightly hysterical giggle. 'Apparently he was expecting a team of porters to be all ready and waiting. Porters! As if I could afford porters. Unbelievable.'

'Ah. I understand completely,' Rick replied, nodding

slowly and scratching his chin, which seemed rather stubblier than he had expected. 'May I make a suggestion?'

She glanced up at him through her eyelashes as she pulled out a cellphone, and sighed out loud. 'Thank you again, but I can manage very well on my own and I am sure that you have some urgent business to attend to. Somewhere else. In the meantime, I need to call a burly bloke moving company. So good morning and have a nice day.'

Rick chuckled under his breath. It was not often that pretty girls gave him the brush-off and maybe a city girl had reasons to be cautious.

'Did your mother tell you not to talk to strangers? Relax. I can spare five minutes to help a lady in distress.'

Her fingers paused and she glared up at him, her eyebrows lifted in disbelief. 'Distress?' There was just enough amusement in her voice to make him take one step forward, but she instantly held up a hand. 'You are mistaken. I am not in distress. I don't do distress. I have never done distress, and I have no intention of starting now. Look.' She popped her phone in her jacket pocket and gingerly wrapped her fingertips around the edge of a pot. And tried to lift it an inch closer.

The pot did not move and she threw a single glance up at him, daring him to say something, but he simply smiled, which seemed to infuriate her even more.

This time she squared her shoulders, gritted her teeth and bent slightly at the knees to go at it again. The pot wobbled slightly then shuddered back to the ground as she hissed in disbelief and stood back with a look on her face as though she wanted to kick the pot hard.

Rick had seen enough. He stepped forward and gently took her arm. 'No need for that. You have all the lifting power you need right here. It's a simple matter of leverage.'

'Leverage!' She laughed and nodded. 'In these shoes? I don't think so.'

'I could move those pots for you. No problem.'

Biting down on her lower lip, the suit looked up at him and he could feel her gaze take in his new Italian boots, denims and leather biker jacket, slowly inching its way up his body until their eyes locked.

And stayed locked.

He watched her expression change as she mentally jostled between necessity and asking for help, which was clearly something she didn't like to do.

Necessity won.

Her tongue flicked out and moistened her lips before she lifted her chin and asked, 'What exactly did you have in mind?'

CHAPTER TWO

Must-Do list
- *Make sure that the new spiral box trees are arranged very elegantly either side of the main entrance. This is bound to impress the clients and set the right tone.*
- *Try and forget how much these two trees cost and watch out for dogs!*
- *Come up with a brilliant plan to shamelessly but unobtrusively use these wine folks to bring in more business.*

IT WAS THE long green twirly plants on sticks that were the problem.

Rick had worked out a way of lifting up the edge of the heavy planter using a wooden door wedge then tipping it forward just enough to use the pot as a lever, but the moment he started to roll the bottom rim of the china pot along on one edge, the plant started waving out of control in all directions across the pavement like some demented flagpole, causing mayhem with the pedestrians.

It was amazing how the street seemed to fill up with girls pushing baby buggies, dog walkers and children in the space of ten minutes, but after two narrow escapes where his secretary had to dodge out of the way or risk getting a tree branch in her eye, Rick had managed to roll one planter all the way from the pavement to the patio without causing serious injury to people or the china base.

'Brilliant,' she gushed, trying to catch her breath after waving away a dog with a full bladder. 'One small step and we're there!'

Rick scratched his chin. 'Tip and shuffle. I tip the pot back and then roll it slightly forward until the edge is on the step. But someone has to hold the greenery out of the way when it swings onto the step. Two man job. Are you up for it?'

He looked up into her face and his breath caught. Close up, he could see that her flawless creamy skin was not a product of pristine grooming and clever make-up but natural beauty which went beyond pretty without being in-your-face gorgeous. The splash of cream at her neck was a perfect contrast to her brown hair and eyebrows and seemed to make her pale blue eyes even more startling.

He had never seen eyes that colour on a girl before but everything about her screamed out that he was talking to a real English rose.

'Absolutely,' she replied with a quick nod and reached for the bottom of the tree. 'Let's do it. Ready? Yes? Go! Oh, ouch. It got me. Almost there. Done!'

Rick stood back, peered at the pot from several angles then leant forward and shifted it to the left slightly.

'That's better.'

'Better! It's fantastic. I don't know what I would have done if you hadn't come along. Thank you so much... Oh, I'm sorry, how rude of me. I don't even know your name...'

'Just call me Rick,' he replied with a wave of one hand. 'And it was my pleasure, Miss...'

'Rick! You found it.'

He half turned as Angie bounded up the pavement towards them, her huge shoulder bag bouncing over one shoulder and a bulging document folder stuffed under her arm and stretched out her hand towards his secretary.

'Miss Elwood, lovely to meet you. Angie Roberts—we talked on the phone earlier. Thanks again for fitting us in at such short notice. What a fabulous house. And I can see that you have already met my boss.'

'Thank you, Angie, and welcome to Elwood House. If you would like to come inside and...' She paused, opened her mouth, closed it again, inhaled slowly and turned back to face him. 'Your boss?'

Rick pushed his shoulders back and glanced sideways at the high gloss painted door of the house whose porch he was standing in. The words 'Elwood House' were engraved in a curvy elegant font on a small brass plaque attached to the stone portico.

It would appear that he had arrived at his destination.

And his English rose was one of the Elwood dynasty.

A low chuckle rumbled in his chest. So this was the hardened old wine merchant he was going to be making his sales pitch to! Well, that showed him. How wrong could he be?

'Rick Burgess.' He grinned into his secretary's stunned face. 'Apparently you are expecting us.'

Rick braced his shoulder on the ornate white marble fireplace in what had been the elegant, huge formal dining room of Elwood House and held the colour brochure for Rick Burgess Wines in one hand as he watched Saskia Elwood glide effortlessly around the sunlit room.

The back split in her slender, elegant pencil skirt fanned open just enough to give him a tantalising glimpse of a pair of very long slender legs above shapely ankles. Not immodest. Oh no. Demure and classy, but tantalising all the same. Just enough to fire up his imagination.

She was impressive.

Every one of his sales team she spoke to looked away from the press release and winemaker portfolios that Angie had passed around to smile up at Saskia and spend a few minutes chatting before going back to their work with that smile still on their lips.

The men and women in the room knew talent when they saw it. Not everyone was able to put a guest instantly at ease. They had expected Saskia to treat them as sales people who were worthy of a cup of instant coffee and a plain biscuit. Well, she had confounded their expectations by treating every one of his four-person team as a guest and potential client in her private meeting venue. Their coffee and tea had been served from silverware with the most delicious homemade pastries and canapés.

Very clever. *He liked clever.* Even if it was obvious to him what she was doing.

His sales people were going to be working with clients from the finest hotels and private homes around London, and Saskia had already worked that out. She might be hosting a sales meeting, but there was no reason why *she* could not sell them the benefits of Elwood House at the same time.

Their hostess was elegant, warm, unpretentious and genuinely interested in her clients. Attentive to their needs, but not intrusive or overfamiliar.

It was precisely what the hospitality industry was all about. And Saskia Elwood had it in spades. He loved watching experts at work. He always had. And the lovely lady of the house was at that moment giving him a master class in exactly the type of customer service he was going to expect in the flagship London face of Burgess Wine.

He glanced back down at his phone. Ten more emails. All from his mother. All wanting urgent updates.

Rick exhaled slowly. A well buried part of his brain knew that she was concerned about him, while the upfront and only too blatant part screamed out a message loud and clear: *They don't think you can pull this off. After two years of hard work you are still the black sheep who is never going to be taken seriously. So you might as well give up now and go back to the sports where you are the best!*

No. Not going to happen. He had made a commitment and he was going to see it through, no matter what it took. Rick Burgess had not risen to the top of his sport by being a quitter.

Strange how his gaze shifted automatically up from the screen towards the slim woman in the pale grey suit, refilling an elegant coffee pot.

Her light brown straight hair was tied loosely back in a shell clip at the base of her neck, which on any other woman would look too casual, but somehow looked exactly right. She knew exactly what she looked like and had taken time to perfect her appearance. Subtle day time make-up, but with skin that clear she didn't need anything but a slick of colour on her lips. This woman knew that her eyes were her best feature and made the best of them. Her eyes were totally riveting. Those eyes captured your attention and held it tight.

Just as they were doing right now as she looked across and flashed him a glance.

Rick slid into a comfortable dining chair and instantly refocused on the business proposal, making notes on the points still to be resolved as he scanned down the snag list. But all the while his left hand tapped out a beat on the fine table and curiosity pricked his skin.

Maybe that was her secret? That hot body that every

man in the room had probably already visualised, which lay under that surface layer of clothing. Tempting the men and impressing the women. She could turn on the heat for the men and the friendly girl power for the ladies.

A clever girl with a hot body wrapped in a teasing and intriguing package.

A frisson of excitement and anticipation sparked across Rick's mind.

It would be quite a coup if he could sign up Margot Elwood's niece to stock his wines and serve them to her guests before the store even opened.

Perhaps that would be the proof he needed to convince his parents that their reckless and, in their eyes, feckless second son would not let them down after all?

Now all he had to do was talk her into it.

Rick glanced around the table. Everyone was seated. They had their promotional material and Saskia was already scanning each page.

The game was on!

'I have just spent the last two years tracking down the finest wine from the new wave of young winemakers all over Europe and persuading them to supply it exclusively to my new flagship wine store right here in central London. Every wine on our list has been personally chosen and vetted.'

'You can say the same thing about every family run wine shop in London, Mr Burgess,' the girl he now knew as Saskia Elwood replied in a light soft voice as her pen tapped onto the cover of his glossy brochure. 'Standards are high.'

'Yes, I know. You heard it all before. But this is new. This is a direct personal connection between the winemaker and the consumer.'

'How confident are you that these new cellars will de-liver?' she asked. 'A new prestigious wine store in the cen-tre of London is one thing, but what assurances can you give me that these winemakers will come back to you year after year? I need to know that I can rely on a guaranteed supply of any wine I add to my list.'

Rick caught her sideways sigh and downward glance but, instead of stomping on her, he grinned and saluted. Her question had not been asked in an angry or accusatory tone. Far from it. She genuinely wanted to hear his answer.

'Great point. What can I give you? My energy and my commitment. I took the time to travel to the vineyards and meet these winemakers. It was not always easy to persuade them to work exclusively with Burgess Wine, but there's one thing I know from my work as a sportsman. Passion recognises passion. These young winemakers have in-vested everything they have because they are obsessive about creating the most amazing wines using modern and traditional techniques. I see that in them. That's why I want to champion these ten small family estates because that is the only way I can guarantee that there will never be such a thing as a boring wine ever again.'

He walked around the table slowly, gesturing to the im-pressive brochure his parents' marketing team had spent weeks perfecting.

'Right now there's a team of marketing experts back in the Californian headquarters for Burgess Wine working on websites for each of the individual growers. When you buy a bottle from this store you will have access to every-thing you need to know about the wine and the passion of the person who made it. I think that's special.'

'Sometimes passion is not enough, Mr Burgess. You need to have the experience and expertise to create a remarkable wine. And these new winemakers are still learning the trade. Not everybody is as...adventurous as you are.'

Rick wrapped his hands around the back of the solid antique dining chair and nodded down the table, making sure that he could capture the attention of Saskia and the three new members of his sales team.

'They don't have to be. The ten growers I've chosen are all part of a mentoring scheme I've created with well-established major winemakers who have been supplying Burgess Wine customers for years. My parents are happy to invest in the wines we select.'

'Don't you mean the wines you select?' Saskia asked with a touch of surprise in her voice. From where he was standing, Rick could see that her gaze was locked onto the back cover of the brochure, which carried an impressive colour photograph of Rick in full climbing gear on a snowy mountain. 'If I am reading this correctly,' she whispered, 'you already have a career as a professional sportsman, Mr Burgess. Does this new store mean that you have turned your back on adventure sports?'

And there it was. Just when he thought he might leave his past behind for a couple of hours and be taken seriously.

Rick pressed the fingers of one hand tight into his palm and fought back his anger. He had to stay frosty.

'Let's just say that I'm focusing on the less hazardous aspects. I haven't broken anything important in years and I have every intention of staying around for a lot longer. So much wine, so little time!'

A ripple of laughter ran around the room but he could almost hear the unspoken question in the air which even his sales team were not prepared to ask out loud but were obviously thinking.

What would happen to this store if Rick Burgess jumped

*off some mountain with a parachute strapped to his back
and the wind caught him and sent him crashing against
the rocks before he could regain control?*

It could happen. In fact it had already happened. One
accident only a few months after Tom died.

How could he forget that day? It had been his first trip
to the mountains since the funeral and he'd needed it as
badly as any other addict needed that cigarette or fix of
their choice.

The oppressive atmosphere of the family home and the
overwhelming grief had finally become too much to bear
and there was only one way he knew to try and get some
balance and peace back into his life. Not trapped in a house
all day staring at the four walls until he wanted to hit a
wall. And go on hitting it until the pain subsided.

He needed to climb a high mountain with a specialised
parachute strapped to his back. He needed to feel the rush
of adrenalin as the wind caught in the parachute and he
felt the power of the air lift him into the sky.

Free. Soaring like a bird. Released from the pain and
trauma and grief of Tom's death.

This was what he did. This was what had taken him to
the awards podium of the European paragliding championships for three years in a row.

And for ten minutes of glorious tranquil flying in long
winding curves he had been precisely where he wanted to
be. Doing what he loved best.

Until one simple gust of wind in the wrong direction
had ruined an otherwise perfect day.

But that was all it had taken to leave him with a broken
collarbone and a badly sprained ankle.

His parents had been shocked and traumatised and full
of complaints about how reckless and uncaring he had

been. How very selfish and irresponsible. But that was nothing compared to the fall in the company credibility in the press.

The media loved to see a reclusive, obsessive sportsman with the golden touch take a fall. And this accident had given them the ammunition they needed to focus on one thing—his lifestyle.

Tom Burgess had been a strategic genius. But his brother Rick? What was he going to bring to the business? He might have taken Tom's seat on the board but maybe the company was taking too much of a risk by bringing in their untrained and reckless second son.

Suddenly major wine producers who had supplied Burgess Wine for years were sucking in their cheeks and wincing about the management team at Burgess Wine.

Never mind the fact that he'd worked tirelessly to be a world-class paraglider and reach the top of this field. Never mind that he was prepared to give the same energy and determination to Burgess Wine and the family business that his brother Tom had transformed into an international company.

Never mind that he had spent the last two years since Tom's death coming up to speed with the business to the point where his family were prepared to even listen to his ideas, despite their misgivings.

Time to make this deal swing his way. Time to take one of those risks he had become famous for. He needed buyers like Saskia Elwood to be interested and excited in this idea, not for himself but for his parents, who had taken a leap of faith. And for every one of the ten small businesses who trusted him with their future.

Rick strolled around the dining table in the sumptuous room towards the head of the table and caught Angie's eye with a quick nod. She instantly slipped out of the room and returned a few minutes later with two silver ice buckets and gently placed them onto silver platters on the fine polished wood table.

'Why don't I let the wine do the talking for me?' Rick smiled and nodded towards the slim wine bottles poking their heads out of the ice buckets. 'Angie tells me that the sample cases are on their way here now, Saskia, but I thought you might like to try something special. A late harvest dessert wine from a single estate in Alsace which is turning out to be one of my favourite discoveries. Are you willing to give it a try?'

'Of course,' Saskia replied, slightly irritated that he thought it appropriate to choose the wine for her. But, as Angie went round the table, pouring the golden liquid into tiny green-tinted glasses, the genuine smiles of appreciation from the men and women in the Burgess sales team as they inhaled the aroma of the wine knocked her sideways.

They might be young but everyone around her table had one thing in common; a real and genuine passion for wine. But did that include the man himself? Her rescuer in denims and the leader of this merry band. Rick Burgess?

Rick sat back down and smiled in encouragement as Angie started a conversation about the Burgundy harvest at the other end of the table while they enjoyed the wine.

Saskia raised the glass of dessert wine to her nose, twirled the glass and inhaled the aroma, which made her eyes flutter in delight and astonishment. Then she sipped the wine ever so slowly.

It was rose petals, musk, vanilla and deep, warm spice. And on the tongue? An explosion of flavour and tingling acidity.

Saskia instantly put down her glass and reached for

the bottle to read the label on the wine bottle. Twenty years old. Rare, exclusive and made by a tiny vineyard she had never heard of in Alsace. It was absolutely delicious. Unique. Expensive. But amazing.

It was so good that this wine could easily have come from the cellars of Elwood Brothers. Her mother and aunt's family had been one of the oldest and most respected wine merchants in Britain, with traditions that went back hundreds of years. The Elwoods were famous around the world for having the finest collection of prestige wines and for employing the leading experts in their field.

Their reputation for quality and excellence had been built up over centuries. It had seemed like the end of a familiar institution when Elwood Brothers finally closed their doors a couple of years ago when the last of the brothers had decided to retire.

It was a shame that she couldn't borrow some of that reputation for excellence to attract more clients to use Elwood House for their board meetings and private dining, combined, of course, with modern technology. The old and the new. The traditional and the modern.

But that was impossible now... Wasn't it?

Saskia felt that familiar prickle of the hairs on the back of her neck as an outrageous and exciting idea gathered shape. Elwood House already had the kudos that came with the name. It would need a lot of investment, but what if she could build up the wine list into one of the finest in London? The best of the old wines and the best of the new.

Perhaps Rick Burgess did have something to offer her after all?

'I am interested to hear your opinion about the wine,' Rick said as he raised his glass towards her. Those grey eyes seemed to almost twinkle as he turned his charm offensive to maximum power. 'I would be a happy man if I can persuade Saskia Elwood to serve my wines to her discriminating and expert guests here in Elwood House. So, tell me. Do I leave here a happy man? Or not?'

CHAPTER THREE

Must-Do list

- *Thank the wine merchant for any free wine they bring. Kate and Amber will be very grateful for the bottles. No promises to buy any, of course.*
- *Canapés. People in the wine trade can eat! Use the sales team as guinea pigs for a couple of new savouries which might work for the Christmas parties. Let them come up with the wine to match— could be interesting.*
- *Do not let this new wine merchant leave without a few of the lovely brochures that Sam worked on. Who knows? Word of mouth recommendation is always the best. They might have some flash customers in need of a private meeting venue.*

BY THE TIME the Burgess Wine sales meeting finally closed, the grey September morning had turned into a bright sunny day. In the light breeze it was still warm enough for the conservatory doors to stay open, and Saskia looked out towards the sales team, who she had invited to finish their coffee on the patio.

The golden coloured flagstones had absorbed the sun and warmed the terrace, creating a welcoming enclosed private garden. Brightly painted Mediterranean-style flowerpots created a soft barrier between the hard stone floor and the exuberant English flower borders and old stone wall covered with fragrant climbing roses and honeysuckle.

This was exactly how she had imagined it would look that cold January when her Aunt Margot had died suddenly, just when she seemed to be recovering from the strokes which had made her life so difficult. Little wonder that these experts in the wine trade were in no hurry to dash out into the rush-hour traffic and fight their way home in this busy part of London.

Saskia glanced quickly over her shoulder towards the table where Rick Burgess and his personal assistant Angie were huddled around a laptop computer.

The strength in Rick's shoulders and back contrasted so fiercely with his long slender fingers. His neck was a twisted rope of sinew as though he was barely holding in a volcano of suppressed energy and power.

This was the man who had effortlessly lifted a planter that morning as though it was weightless.

She had felt such an idiot when Angie had arrived and her knight in denim and a leather jacket had turned out to be the client that she had been waiting for.

It had so totally floored her that she had felt off balance for most of the morning. Not that she would ever let him know that, of course.

The company directors she met did not usually turn up to meetings wearing clothes more suited to a motorcycle rally. In fact she wouldn't be surprised in the least if there was some huge, hulking two-wheeled machine parked around the corner at that minute, waiting for him to leap on and roar away.

Combine that with tousled dark curly hair and designer stubble.

Rick Burgess was certainly a company director with a difference.

She watched him stand and share a laugh with Angie as they gathered up their papers and, just for a fraction of a second, she wondered what it would be like to be on the receiving end of the full-on charm of that power smile that beamed out of a rugged, handsome face.

She knew that she had never been the pretty one, or super-creative or musically talented like her best friends Kate and Amber. But it would be nice now and again to have a handsome man really look at her as a woman and like what he saw. Instead of asking where the toilets were and could he have more coffee.

Her beautiful mother Chantal had often said that Saskia had skipped a generation and would be much happier back in rural France on the vineyard where her own mother had been brought up, instead of living the high life of a city girl.

And she was right in so many ways.

Her mother could never understand why the teenage Saskia had begged to spend the school holidays working at the *auberge* with her extended French family instead of sitting on some tropical beach with her mother and her friends, while her father stayed in his room and worked on some financial deal or other.

Of course that was when her grandparents were alive and her parents were still together. When her father left them everything changed.

Suddenly her practical skills were useful and Saskia became the girl who made sure that there was food in the refrigerator and the bills were paid as her mother struggled to come to terms with what had happened and failed. Saskia had never once missed school or turned up without a clean uniform and brushed hair. When her mother's world imploded she had become the dependable one who made sure things happened.

The girl who would always help you out at the last minute.

Not done your homework? Ask Saskia to help. All you had to do was pretend to be her friend, just long enough to get what you wanted.

It had been a long apprenticeship forged from hard times, but, like it or not, fifteen years of training and hard work in the hotel and food trade had brought her to this point. She should be happy, ecstatic really, but all this was hers and she had made the business feasible on her own.

Not that there was any choice. Without Elwood House, she would be working for someone else. She couldn't go back to that. Not ever.

Not after she had promised her aunt that she would take care of the house and make all of their great plans a reality.

It was worth the exhaustion and never-ending strive for excellence.

As the Burgess sales team moved into the hall, Saskia pressed her fingertips hard against the fine marble surface of the console table and took a deep breath before lifting her chin and personally thanking each of them in turn as they left the building, discreetly counting to make sure that no one had got locked in the washroom or had decided to take an unsupervised tour of the bedrooms upstairs.

She sensed rather than heard someone coming up to speak to her and she spun around. 'Miss Elwood. Could you spare a moment?'

Up close and personal, Rick Burgess was just as physically impressive standing in her hallway as he had been on the pavement that morning. Even after two hours of what had been sometimes intense discussions, back and forth across the table, the intelligence in his grey eyes sparkled with life and vigour against a tanned face which had never seen a tanning salon.

'Of course,' she replied. 'How can I help, Mr Burgess?'

'Oh, please call me Rick,' he replied and stretched out his hand to shake Saskia's. 'I just wanted to say a huge thank you for agreeing to see us today. We appreciate your time and your warm welcome into your lovely home.'

'I am delighted that you enjoyed it.' She sucked in a breath when he released his grip, which was a lot firmer than she was used to. As in finger-crushing firmer. 'If you should ever need a venue for a business meeting, I do hope that you will consider Elwood House.'

'A business meeting?' His eyebrows rose and, as he returned her smile, the deep tan lines at the corners of his mouth and eyes creased into sharp falls. 'Sure. My project team will need to get together every few weeks during pre-launch. Angie will get in contact. Although I do have one request before I take off.'

His hands pushed into the pockets of his denims. 'Prepare to be shocked. I am about to declare a terrible failing.'

'A failing?' Saskia replied, trying not to smile. 'Surely not.'

Rick sighed out loud and raised both hands in the air. 'I can understand that such a thing is hard to believe but here it is.' He paused for dramatic effect and stepped just a little closer than she was comfortable with. 'I'm not known for my patience. There were a couple of times during the presentation that I picked up some sense that you might be interested in buying from me. Am I right?'

'Ah. Well, now it is my turn for confession,' Saskia replied, her gazed locked onto his face. 'I try not to make snap decisions when it comes to spending my money. My late aunt, Margot Elwood, taught me that loyalty to a supplier means a very great deal. I am therefore rather cautious about who I give my loyalty to, and one bottle of wine is no guarantee that the others will be of the same quality.'

'Loyalty. I like that idea.'

Rick glanced over Saskia's shoulder. 'How about I give my future loyal customer a hand and carry that box of sample bottles down to her wine cellar? Who knows? I might pick up a few tips from an Elwood.'

'My wine cellar?' Saskia repeated. 'I'm very flattered—' she smiled '—thank you, but I am sure it would be boring compared to the wonderful wines you have in your stockrooms. And I am quite capable of carrying a few bottles down a corridor.'

Saskia straightened and kept her smile firmly fixed as she gazed past Rick Burgess towards the front door. 'I wouldn't want to keep your team waiting.'

Rick replied by tilting his head. 'They're already heading back to the office. So you see, Miss Elwood, I'm all yours. Now. Where do you want me to put this box?'

'I store the specialist wine and ports in the basement. Oh, and please mind your head. These old cellars were built for shorter people.'

Rick followed Saskia down the narrow stone steps that led from her modern stainless steel kitchen down into the brick and stone storeroom and cellar that ran almost the full length of the house. He carefully lowered the large cardboard box of wine onto a sturdy old wooden table before following her into the cellar.

Saskia flicked on the lighting system and started her tour with the classic red wines she had bought for the coming autumn and winter season before moving on to the older and more prestigious wines. Racks and racks of bottles were laid out on their sides in purpose-built curved trays, label up, creating a superb display.

Rick peered politely at each of the winemakers and vintages with only a quick nod to indicate that he was only vaguely interested in what he was looking at.

It was not just annoying, it was unsettling!

She was just about to turn back when Rick pointed towards the cabinet where she stored her most precious white wines, most of which she had inherited from her aunt.

'I recognise that wine, it's one of my father's favourites.'

'Then we have something in common.' She smiled. 'It's one of my favourites too. It also happens to be made at the vineyard once owned by my Elwood grandparents. Yes, that's right. This is my family wine.'

'Ah—' Rick chuckled '—you see. I was right—I have learnt something new. Although it does make me wonder why you don't promote your connection to the famous Elwood family more on your website. That is a remarkable heritage to be proud of.'

She replied by smiling and shaking her head. 'There is a very good reason for that. I might be an Elwood but I have never been a wine merchant and I wouldn't want anyone coming here under false pretences.'

Rick strolled up, pressed his shoulder snugly against hers and dropped his gaze onto a copy of a wine label that she was holding in her hand. His long wide mouth curved up into a smile that raised the temperature of the air in the cellar by several degrees. 'I know about that.' He chuckled. 'Here I am, with a new career as a wine merchant and about to open a new wine store. Everything I know about the business I picked up from a lifetime living with a family who is obsessed with everything to do with wine.'

'Aunt Margot may have been the last of the Elwood family but there was nothing that you could tell that lady about wine. I only wish I had her experience and knowledge.'

'Exactly!' Rick said in a voice bubbling with enthusiasm. 'This is why I need to be totally honest with you about the real reason that I am here today.'

'Real reason? What do you mean?'

His reply was to move closer, stretch out one long muscular arm to the stone wall behind her shoulder and lean forward so that their faces were only inches apart. Trapping her in the space between his body and the wine racks, which were pressing into her back.

Any closer and she would be on intimate terms with his shirt buttons.

She could hunch down and dive under his armpit if she had a mind to but this was her cellar, not his. And, damn him, but she was not the one who was going to have to move first. Even if he did smell of soft leather and fine wine underpinned by a faint citrus tang of some no doubt very expensive male grooming product designed to act as instant girl attractor.

And Lord, it was worth every penny he had spent.

His gaze scanned her face for several too long seconds before he whispered and stepped so close that she could almost feel the heat of his breath on her brow. 'I think you are being far too modest, Saskia. From what I've seen today, the clients who come to Elwood House are lucky enough to have the very best and the excellent taste of the *mistress* of this fine house.'

The way Rick lingered on that last word sent shivers up her spine which she blinked away. Was he trying to flirt with her?

As for modest? What choice did she have? Her mother might have fled to Los Angeles, leaving her with her aunt, but it was her father who had truly ripped her heart out. She never mentioned him to anyone, not even Kate or Amber. She had even changed her surname the same week her mother had finally agreed to a divorce and went back to being Chantal Elwood again. But he was always there at the back of her mind. A constant itch that could never be scratched away. Reminding her to be careful and not take risks, no matter how tantalising they might appear.

Saskia lifted her chin slightly. She had to stay professional. Even if he was totally inside her comfort zone and oozing enough testosterone to make her forget her own name.

'Just this.' He breathed low and hoarse, his head tilted slightly to one side. 'What would you say if I was prepared to sign a contract committing Rick Burgess Wines to hold a lunch meeting at least every week right here in Elwood House for the next two years?'

He paused and let the silence create the anticipation he was looking for.

'What would I say?' Saskia repeated, lifting her chin slightly sideways so that she could smile up into his face without straining her back. 'I would say thank you very much and here is a piece of paper and a pen.'

'I thought that you might. But there is a catch.'

'Am I going to like it?'

'Like it? I hope so. You see, my company specialises in exciting wine made by a whole new wave of brilliant new winemakers from right across Europe. I need customers like you to take a risk and invest in these wines. But one short presentation is not nearly long enough. So...' his hips shifted slightly, just in case she had not noticed how tight his jeans were, stretched over his muscular thighs '...I was hoping that you might be available to have dinner with me this evening. It would give me a chance to tell you more about what I had to offer. If you were free.'

Free? She was free for dinner every evening.

Rick was smiling at now, but she could see the muscles in his lower arm move slightly as they adjusted to a shift in his position. Dark brown hair curled onto broad muscular shoulders. Sinewy neck and jaw. Beyond rugged, physical and potent.

Butterflies fluttered in the pit of her stomach under the intensity of that gaze and she had the sudden urge to toss her hair back, stick her chest out and flirt with him outrageously. His dark blue-grey eyes shone bright in the low light she used in the cellars to protect the wine. There was a certain slight unease around his lips as though he wanted to say something, reveal something, but thought better of it and held back.

What he had to offer? Oh, she had a pretty good idea. *Dangerous.*

Buying wine from him? *Oh no.* Fingers. Hot. Burnt.

Suddenly she felt a desperate urge to fill the silence with chatter.

'Building a reputation for excellence takes time. I only opened up the house to guests a few months ago and I cannot afford to risk my reputation by serving any else but the best.'

'Absolutely.' He nodded. 'This is why I think my business proposition might just solve both of our problems rather neatly. My wonderful wines. Your fine reputation. Perfect fit.'

She paused and licked her lips. 'I don't want to seem rude, but my clients expect the very best and it's my job to make sure that they are not disappointed. But don't worry, Angie has given me her contact details and has promised to be in touch about any future business meetings. I look forward to seeing you again at Elwood House.'

Saskia stretched out her hand towards Rick and he glanced at it for a second before moving back, chuckling and wrapping his fingers around hers.

'People don't usually turn me down,' he whispered,

stepping forward under the spotlight until he was far enough away for Saskia to see the fine white scar lines that ran up one side of his face. 'I'm curious. Are you always so sceptical? What do you want to know? Ask me anything during our dinner this evening and I'll promise that I will tell you the truth.'

Saskia was still reeling from his reply when Rick's cellphone blared out a top ten music track and he glanced quickly at the caller ID, breaking the intensity of the moment.

'You seem very confident that you have something that I might be interested in, Mr Burgess. Perhaps you could ask Angie to make an appointment for later in the week.'

'Nope. Has to be tonight. I'll pick you up at seven.'

Pick her up. Oh no. This was not a date. She had to take some control back!

'I sometimes walk along the South Bank around half seven,' she gushed before her brain had time to engage.

'Got it. Later.'

Two fingers to the forehead in a quick salute and he turned on his heel and strolled away to the stairs as if he owned the place, leaving a Rick-sized space in her cellar.

He hadn't waited for her answer.

The strange thing was; she couldn't remember saying no.

Saskia peered at her reflection in the screen of her smartphone, wiggled her head from side to side several times and pushed several stands of hair behind her ear. Large ornate drop earrings in the shape of a leaf swung freely in the late sunshine, reflecting back the light from the finely worked Indian silver.

'Thanks, Amber. Those earrings are just perfect. I love them. You are a genius when it comes to style. What's that?

Takes one to know one. Well, thank you, kind lady. And don't forget to thank Kate for the loan of her jacket. The colours work so well together.'

She glanced quickly around the busy pavement to check that her quiet smirk had gone unseen. 'Amber! Stop that. You are making me blush. Those earrings are staying on. This is not a hot date. I keep telling you. Business meeting. Stop laughing. Business! And no, I don't want you to wait up for me. Cheek! Now go and be creative with the wedding plan. Talk to you later if you must. Later. Yes. Okay. I promise that I will have a nice time. Thank you. Yes.'

Saskia chuckled out loud and flipped her phone closed. Kate and Amber had just spent over an hour helping her come up with the perfect outfit but, she had to admit, her style consultants had pulled together a smart but casual look which created just the right impression.

Neat wraparound plain navy dress, smart designer jacket, which Kate had run back to her studio to collect at the last minute, discreet jewellery and medium heels which she knew that she could walk in, just in case Rick turned up in his boots again and took off across London on foot.

She was determined to show Rick that she was a professional to the core and not just another girl who he could order around on a whim.

This was meeting a client for drinks away from Elwood House.

Not a date or meeting a friend. This was a business meeting with a potentially large booking in the balance.

Just because she had agreed to go out for drinks did not mean that she was saying yes. It was simply playing fair and giving him a chance to discuss this mysterious business proposal.

Wasn't it?

Of course she was intrigued—how could she not be?

What did he think he could offer that the wonderful London wine merchants could not?

Nothing to do with that molten chocolate voice and dark blue-grey eyes. Oh no. She was not going down that road.

The man was a maniac. A riveting, passionate, handsome charmer of a maniac.

Who was clever enough to dangle something he knew that she might be interested in, but hold it just beyond her reach.

How did he expect professionals to take him seriously if he turned up in denims and leather and barely shaven? Did he really not care what he looked like? Or was he simply playing a trick and acting out a persona created by the company PR department?

Squaring her shoulders, Saskia pushed back from the railing and glanced along the Thames Embankment in the fading September sunshine.

And froze. Because strolling towards her on the wide pavement was Rick Burgess. No entourage, no team, just Rick. Wearing exactly the same clothes that she had last seen him in.

His hips swung out with each stride, purposefully and in line with the rock-solid body under those tight denims.

Every inch of his body screamed out confidence and self-belief. He could fit in anywhere he went and, judging by the backwards glances from the ladies he passed with each purposeful and determined step, it was a look which guaranteed him an audience.

And, just like that, she got it.

Rick truly did not care one bit what other people thought about his appearance.

He dressed to please himself and if the rest of the world did not like it—that was not his problem.

This was no act designed to provoke a reaction or a

cheap media gimmick to attract some extra press cover-
age because he was so deliberately different from other
wine merchants in the city.

He was Rick.

Take it or leave it. That was him.

No artifice, no pretence, no insincere gestures to pla-
cate his audience.

He knew who he was and was totally happy inside his
skin.

He was the real deal.

It blew her away. And terrified her so much that it was
not even vaguely funny.

Rick Burgess was exactly the kind of sex on legs man
that she had been avoiding since the day her dad was arrested. She knew the type and she had tasted what it felt
like to be consumed by the fire on the altar of their all-
powerful ego. And she never wanted to be burnt alive
again.

The problem was, back in Elwood House she'd been
surrounded by the familiar rooms and furniture and high-
tech presentation equipment and other people.

They were her security screen.

But at that minute in this public street she felt as though
they might as well have been the only two people on the
Embankment that evening, with not even Aunt Margot's
dining table between them.

Her gaze simply could not move away from that powerful dark face as he strode towards her. It was as though
he had a huge magnet which was pulling them closer and
closer together, making it impossible for her to break the
connection.

All of the carefully worded and highly professional re-
fusals and excuses she had planned in the kitchen when
she was clearing away vanished from her brain, wiped out

by the stunningly relaxed and sexy-as-hell smile he was giving her. The corner of one side of his mouth lifted as he strolled closer, creating crease lines in his cheeks and the corners of his eyes.

Perhaps she should have looked Rick Burgess up on the Internet instead of cleaning the house and polishing it back to perfection. It might have given her some ammunition to fire at him and scare him away.

Which was what she wanted...wasn't it?

To politely turn him down while still keeping the bookings.

What other reason could there possibly be?

So why did she find it so difficult to lift her chin and take the few steps to close the distance between them?

'Nice earrings.'

'Nice boots.'

He smiled and replied with a small shoulder shrug. 'My mother told me that I should smarten myself up before the meeting today. And, like the good boy that I am, I always do what my mother tells me.'

She replied by raising her eyebrows. A good boy? She doubted that very much.

Her silent gesture must have hit home because he strolled forward and startled her by nudging her ever so gently along one side of her arm.

It was the touch of a friend, not someone she had just met.

How much more outrageous could he get?

Then that amazing wide mouth broadened into a smirk of a smile and his grey eyes focused on the river.

'Yeah, I concede that one. Maybe not a good boy all of the time. But hey. It's nice to have something to aim for. As you know. But let's not talk about business. Not yet, anyway. This is way too nice an evening.'

He sniffed and looked around. 'You know, it's been years since I was on the South Bank. But, as it happens, I know a family-run Tuscan restaurant right on the river you might enjoy. Willing to risk it?'

Risk it? No, thank you. She gave up on risk a long time ago. Not when she had experienced first-hand the fallout from other people taking risks they should not have.

On the other hand, there was no point arguing in public with a company director who could put Elwood House into profit with one contract.

She could risk his choice of restaurant for a few hours, even if it did turn out to be a kebab shop.

'That sounds perfect. Do you need a map?'

'Maps? Maps are for people who don't know where they are going. Where is the fun in that? Oh no,' he said and, without asking permission, he took hold of her hand and looped it over the crook of his arm, capturing her and holding her tight. 'Let's rock.'

CHAPTER FOUR

Must-Do list

- *This is NOT a date—simply drinks and dinner with a prospective client. Stay charming and professional at all times. Do NOT flirt with the handsome man who wants you to buy his wine. He probably has a lovely wife and family back home. Ignore any advice from Kate and Amber on dating techniques.*
- *Do not panic or blurt out your life story if the conversation flags.*
- *Keep your taxi money handy—you will be going home alone.*

TWENTY MINUTES LATER Saskia strolled out of the ladies' room at a wonderful Italian restaurant she hadn't known existed until that evening, just in time to see Rick being back-slapped by the rotund father of the family while Rick chatted away in fluent Italian to the two sons who took care of the bar and waiter service on a Monday evening.

He might have been part of their family.

How had he done that?

The other diners in the packed restaurant were certainly enjoying whatever story he was regaling them with.

In fact they were almost disappointed when Rick broke

off mid-anecdote to go back to their window table and pull out a chair for her.

It was strange how the most delicious-smelling piping-hot rosemary and olive foccacia suddenly appeared on the table with a bottle of the best wine on the list, which the owner himself insisted on opening and checking before pouring Saskia a generous glass and then he turned to Rick, who joined in the joke. He swirled the glass with an over the top swagger, inhaled and then guffawed with appreciation—which led to even more waving of arms and laughter from the kitchen area.

Rick turned back to Saskia and raised his glass. 'Your health, lovely lady. This food smells good. Mind if I go first?'

'Dive in. Okay, I am impressed. You speak excellent Italian for an American wine merchant.'

'Born in Scotland, moved to Napa aged twelve, but spend most of my time in the French Alps close to the Italian border,' Rick replied between bites of foccacia. 'I might have picked up a few words. And this is great. Try some.'

'Thank you, I will,' she replied and sat back and looked around the restaurant for a few seconds. The stress of the day, the week and the month seemed to ease away in this cosy atmosphere. She felt her shoulders drop as she relaxed and enjoyed the moment.

'That must have been difficult,' she whispered.

'Difficult?' Rick looked up.

'Moving to another country when you were twelve must have meant leaving your friends and relatives behind. Not easy for a young person.'

He opened his mouth, paused and then closed it again, his gaze scanning her face. 'No—' he shrugged after several minutes '—it wasn't easy at all. But my parents and older brother helped me settle into a new life. Of course, once I saw what the sports facilities were like I had a great time.'

'Modest too. Well, it seems that you are full of surprises, Mr Burgess.'

He chuckled and shook his head. 'Mr Burgess is my dad. I only answer to Rick. Okay? And I'm pleased that you like it.'

She waved one hand daintily in the air and tore off a piece of bread and popped it into her mouth.

And the explosion of flavour hit her hard.

Wow.

She looked over Rick's shoulder at the patron, who winked at her from the bar.

Winked.

'Do you know,' she managed, between more bites, 'I have been eating in Italian restaurants all over London with my aunt since I was ten years old and this is the best foccacia that I have eaten, and the wine...' she picked up the bottle and peered at the label '...is from a tiny estate just north of Florence. I have been trying to persuade them to supply me for months. It's fantastic.'

'Wait until you taste the fresh pasta with anchovy and tomato sauce. Mario's mother is in there making it herself, just for us.'

'How? Why? Or do you normally have this effect on complete strangers?'

He smiled and rested his elbows on the table so that he could lean forward into her space.

'The recommendation came from Mario's nephew and his new young wife. Yesterday morning I was putting together a business plan for their fledgling winemaking operation a few miles closer to the sea from where this wine was made. It's going to mean a lot of hard work but the vines are old and run deep in the poor soil. They are going to go places. And the family are right behind them.'

Then he leant back. 'They are just one of ten young winemakers who will have their work showcased by RB Wines. They're excited, I'm excited. You see, I am buying all of their wine. Every last bottle. I am their only customer and I have signed a contract to say that their wine will only be available from one shop. The flagship store I am opening in the spring.'

'But Burgess Wine is a huge online operation. Doesn't it make more sense to sell their wine around the world?'

'You're right.' Rick shrugged. 'My family have worked hard to expand the online wine business to cover most of the West Coast of America. But not Europe. Plus these growers are only making a few hundred cases every year at most, which is not nearly enough for the online trade. Different style. Different market. Different customers. They are taking a risk, of course. If I can't sell their wine in London...' He flipped his hands into the air in a very Mediterranean style.

'You go broke and so do they.' Saskia sighed out loud and took another long sip of wine. 'You are asking prospective customers like me to spend money on an unknown winemaker based solely on your recommendation and hoping we are happy with the results. That is one brave marketing plan.'

'I suppose that is what it comes down to in the end, yes.'

'I see,' she whispered and focused her complete attention on the crumbs left in the bread basket, her lips pressed tight together.

A roar of laughter rang out from the man across the table and she sprang back and looked up into Rick's face. His whole body was shaking and he had to wipe away the tears from his eyes before shaking his head and grinning at her.

'Please promise me that you will never take up a career as a poker player. Oh dear, the look on your face was priceless.'

'I am delighted to have provided you with such amusement,' she sniffed.

His response was to reach across the table, pick up her hand and kiss her knuckles before lowering it back to the table.

'I'm not laughing at you—' he smiled '—just your reaction. It was the perfect confirmation of what I already suspected. Did you really think that I picked these winemakers out of the phone book by closing my eyes and sticking a pin at random on the pages?'

He narrowed his eyes and shook his head slowly from side to side. 'It has taken me two years of tracking down a shortlist of growers based on word of mouth recommendation from people I trust in the business. Then I spent my time and money sending in a team of experts who can pull together a complex combination of geology and climate and do all of the background checks before we went to the vineyard and met them in person. These are not ten random growers. They are the future stars of the winemaking world. And I got there first.'

He tilted his head to one side. 'But you don't see that when you look at me. Do you? You don't see the work and the long hours that go on behind the scenes. You see Rick the maverick sportsman.'

He held up his hands as she tried to bluster a response. 'Well, do you know what? A few years ago you would have been right. I didn't come into the wine trade by choice. But once I make a commitment to do something, I stick to it.'

Rick tipped his head towards her. 'I do things my way.

I don't stick to the rules and dance to someone else's tune. I know who I am and I know what I want. And sometimes people have a hard time coming to terms with that.'

He switched on that killer smile that left no doubt at all in her mind that he was used to getting precisely what he wanted, from any female of any age in a hundred yard radius.

'Now, I am talking too much about myself. It took me a few minutes to make the connection between Elwood House and the Elwood Brothers wine merchants. I only went there once—' Rick saluted with his bread '—and it was an education. Shame it closed. Professional curiosity. Where do you buy the wine for those cellars you showed me today? Not from Burgess Wine—I checked.'

'From the growers, mostly. Aunt Margot was quite a character and there was a time when Elwood House was a sort of unofficial bed and breakfast hotel for any passing winemaker who was in town. She had an address book other wine merchants could only dream of.'

'Add me to that list. That must have been an amazing experience.'

'Oh, it was—I was sent to bed early on many occasions when things were getting a little too jolly in the kitchen, if you know what I mean. There are some real eccentrics in the wine business. Luckily for me, they kept in touch after she passed and they're still willing to ship me their best vintages at market prices. The clients certainly appreciate the quality.'

'I can vouch for that. Do you still talk to the Elwood side of your family?'

'I am sorry to say that I am the last of the line and my mother has her own life.' Saskia looked up from her glass. 'What about your parents? Burgess Wine is based in California now, isn't it?'

'Aha. So I am not the only one who hit the Internet today. No need to blush. You already know the office is in the Napa Valley. A long way from central Scotland where they started, but it's where the wine producers are based so it makes perfect sense. And the climate is slightly better.'

'Just a bit,' Saskia replied, feeling a lot more relaxed when he was talking about his family and not hers. 'Oh, my goodness. Look at that!'

Rick sat back in his chair opposite Saskia and watched her inhale the aroma of the huge bowl of the most delicious pasta, then turn to the chef with a grin and chatter away in perfect Italian, much to Mama's delight, who couldn't wait to share the recipe.

Apparently, adding a ladle of the pasta water to the sauce made all the difference!

It was worth letting his cheese melt just to look at her.

He had half expected Saskia to wear her business suit and a body armour type of corset, but instead he was enjoying dinner with a girl who could have been poured into a wrap dress which clung to all of the right places and gave a man just enough of a tantalising glimpse of what lay beneath to click the right buttons.

Combine that with a brain and an attitude which made him stay awake and pay attention and he was more than interested in Saskia Elwood the woman as well as the heir to the Elwood name.

At Elwood House she was the body in a suit which he couldn't resist. But here? Here, she was a knockout.

Not that he would ever admit it, of course, but it had thrown him when Saskia had asked about his move to California as a boy.

How could he possibly explain to this girl just how tough it had been? Anger at the injustice of being dragged away from everything he knew and having no say at all in the decision was the one common emotion he remembered only too well from those terrible first few years. It hadn't helped that his elder brother Tom had been the seventeen-year-old genius who'd excelled in every academic subject he'd turned to at their new high school in California.

Not that he blamed Tom for being the academic son in the family. That was who he was. But the brighter Tom's star had shone, the more the young Rick Burgess had become a damp firework. And the more the teachers and other pupils had compared him to Tom, the angrier he had become at the injustice and ridicule he had to endure.

Pity that his parents had been too busy working every hour of the day to build a new online wine business to notice that their second son was desperately unhappy.

But he had been honest with Saskia about the sports. Without a physical outlet for his suppressed anger and resentment, he could have turned that energy into something far more damaging.

Saskia waved at Mario and Rick joined in the laughter for a moment before tucking into his food.

Perhaps it was not so surprising that Saskia had picked up on that part of his life?

Angie had come up with so much background material on the Elwood family that he had barely had time to skim-read the essentials when they'd got back to the London office. But one thing was clear. Saskia Elwood Mortimer had become Saskia Elwood for a very good reason. *Her father.*

It had taken him all of five minutes to work out that Hugo Mortimer would not be winning any prizes as a father and a husband and as a property developer he was a disaster. Dropping the Mortimer name made sense for a teenage girl who was the daughter of a man whose embezzlement scandal hit the headlines around the world. Worse, it was an investment scam that had finally taken him to the law courts and a long prison sentence in an American jail.

Saskia Elwood had every reason to be cautious around men with big ideas and bigger promises.

He got that. Better than she might imagine. He was not Tom. But he shared Tom's drive and determination to do what he had to in order to achieve his goals. He always had.

It was time to get creative and do something nobody expected him to do.

He had spent most of his life pushing the boundaries and asking forgiveness later; much to his parents' despair.

Life was not for hanging around waiting for other people to give him permission.

And he had absolutely no intention of changing that philosophy any time soon, even if that meant cutting corners a little when it came to making his store a triumph of innovation and excitement.

Direct action. No more talking and a lot more walking.

He was going to show Saskia Elwood that he meant business and she could trust him to deliver on his promises in the only way he knew how, up front and personal.

All he had to do was find some way of persuading her to leave her cosy little nest and jump on the morning flight back to France.

Persuading women to agree to his every whim was usually not a problem for him. Shame that Saskia was not the type of woman he normally met. He liked girls who could stand up for themselves and make their own way. Running a private meeting venue on your own was not a trivial thing. He admired her for that.

But, from what he had seen today, there was something she wanted. Something that he could give her. Something she might find too irresistible to turn down.

'It's good to see a girl enjoying her food,' he quipped as

Saskia liberally tossed cheese and black pepper over the generous portion of pasta that she had piled into her bowl.

Her hand froze, then relaxed as he chuckled quietly under his breath and loaded his bowl with twice her portion.

'Guilty as charged. I love my food and drink. Always have.'

'Well, here is a thought. How you would like to travel to France with me tomorrow? It shouldn't take more than three or four days to visit each of the vineyards, but I guarantee that you will be back here for Monday morning.'

'France? Why would I want to go to France with you?'

Rick waggled his eyebrows a couple of times up and down and then grinned when she groaned and turned back to her food with a shake of her head.

'I fell into that one.' She waved. 'Please. Carry on.'

'Apart from the pleasure of your delightful company, I thought that you might be persuaded to buy wine from me if you met some of the producers in person.'

'Ah. Emotional blackmail. Once I meet the growers you know that I will not be able to say no to them. Now that is a low trick.'

He paused and took a sip of wine before looking up at Saskia. He knew all about emotional blackmail. His parents were experts.

'Not at all. Creating my own business means that I have the freedom to create my own list of premium customers. Customers like you.'

Her head came slowly up and she continued chewing for a moment before replying, 'Me? I don't think so.'

'But I do. I want you to be part of that first wave of special buyers in London, Saskia. No. More than that. I need you to support my launch. In return, I am offering you an amazing discount on the wine and I will promote Elwood House along the way. That is special.'

'Why do you want to sell to a one-woman operation like me?' she replied with a short cough of disbelief. 'Why not focus on the big five-star hotels where you can be guaranteed large orders?'

Rick swallowed down his pasta and waved the fingers of one hand towards her chest. 'Because of who your family are, of course. I want the Elwood name to be attached to my store. It's as simple as that.'

She stared at him in shocked silence as though she could hardly believe what she had heard. So he continued to twirl his linguini and talk at the same time. 'My parents sign contracts with bulk producers over slick boardroom tables without even visiting the vineyard. I cannot work like that. No. I refuse to work like that.'

Risk shook his head. 'I deal with people one to one. When they sign a contract they are signing it with me, not some faceless organisation who will drop them at the first sign of trouble. I am the person who commits to making their dream come true and in return they make the best wine that they are capable of. And that is something very special. Something you can be part of.'

He scanned the table for a second then pounced on the bowl of Parmesan, deliberately ignoring the fact that Saskia was glaring at him with a look that could freeze ice.

He brushed his hands off and pushed the bowl across the table to her abandoned dinner. 'More Parmesan? No? It is quite simple really. I meant what I said earlier. You want to serve the best. And I believe that I have the best. Come to France with me tomorrow and I'll show you why I'm sticking my neck out. No glossy brochures, no fancy advertising agencies. Just a hands-on demonstration of the quality RB Wines is going to become world famous for. That way we both win!'

Saskia slid back in her chair and folded her arms. 'So let me get this straight. You want me to buy wine from you so that you can use the Elwood name as some sort of seal of approval for your producers. You don't need me at all. You just need the name to bring some credibility to a risky business venture. Isn't that more like the truth?'

'Oh, I want a lot more than that,' he replied as he lowered his wine glass. 'I want to buy credibility and respectability with a huge dollop of tradition and heritage on the side.'

His fingers traced out a sign in the air between them. 'RB Wines. Suppliers to Elwood House, London. It would give me just the kudos to bring customers in the door, and, once inside the shop, we can create the most tantalising selection of prestige wines in the city. Which you get to see first. The best for the best.'

'*We* can create the selection of wines? I'm not sure I believe that. Not when the mighty Richard Burgess ego is part of the decision making process. It's almost as if you want to become the new Elwood Brothers but all on your own.'

He paused then slowly nodded his head. 'Yes, I suppose I do.' A strange look crossed Rick's face and he chuckled at the back of his throat. 'Now that is one hell of a crazy thought. Yeah. Actually that is amazing. Thank you.'

'In fact, you have a brother, don't you?'

He looked up at her as though he had temporarily forgotten that she was there.

'Not any longer. But that doesn't matter. RB Wines is going to be spectacular.'

She unfolded her arms and leant forward and stared at him in the eyes. He didn't even blink or look away.

'This is a vanity project, Richard Burgess. And I'm not interested in pandering to your ego by selling out my family name. Not for any money.'

'Selling out your name? Oh no, that's not what I'm offering. I haven't got to the good bit yet.'

'Oh, there's a good bit? Well, please carry on. This should be most entertaining.'

He put down his fork and bent from the waist so that their noses were almost touching. 'I don't want to buy your name, Saskia. I'm offering you the chance to take the inside track on the best new producers in Europe and, as a bonus, my company will commit to using Elwood House for the next two years. Now that's what I call a partnership made in heaven.'

Of all the arrogance!

Saskia glared at Rick and decided that she must be hearing things.

Otherwise, this casually dressed hotshot had just demanded that she drop everything and take off to France with him for a few days. With the promise of a long-term meeting contract—if she agreed to buy and, more importantly to her, serve his wine to her clients, who expected her to give them the best.

RB Wines would be sitting on her shelves next to a handful of growers who had been supplying the Elwood family for decades and, in the case of some chateaux, for over a century.

As if flashing his money around would open the doors to the cellars. Hah!

She had grown up surrounded by people who thought that arrogance and bravado could get them where they wanted to go. Charming, attractive people like her father, who believed that they could do what they liked and tell people what to do and get away with it.

Her father was not so different from Rick.

Handsome, tall, dark, with wonderful eyes and a smile that could disarm a woman the minute she laid eyes on him and persuade even the hardest businessmen into handing over their money and investing in commercial property in cities all over the world.

And they had.

Shame that her father thought that using other people's money to pay for his high risk building projects was a perfectly acceptable thing to do. He was arrogant enough to believe that he couldn't fail and his plans for office buildings designed by cutting-edge architects had become risky and riskier. *Blame the property market,* he used to say, *not me. Just wait until the economy picks up. Companies will be desperate to use my office space and everyone will get a great return on their money.*

It had come as quite a shock when the courts disagreed.

Saskia remembered only too clearly what it was like for her mother on the day he'd been arrested for embezzlement and fraud. She'd believed in him, trusted him and had faith in all his excuses and rational explanations for why they were losing money day after day.

They had both loved him so badly that the truth was hard to accept. He was a fool. An arrogant and delusional man who thought that money could buy him status and class and power. That was why he'd married her mother. Chantal Elwood was the only daughter of one of the famous Elwood brothers, the most respected wine merchant in Britain. And the oldest. The Elwood family had given him access to clients he would never have otherwise met.

Little wonder that they'd trusted Hugo Mortimer when he came to them with an idea for a thirty-storey office block in a mid-west American city. *Trust me,* he'd said. *These buildings are going to be safe havens for your money in the current financial climate.* And they had trusted him.

And he had abused the power and influence and robbed them and cheated them.

She yearned to tell Rick exactly what he could do with his proposal but she couldn't.

'A partnership made in heaven?' She gulped. 'Well, your idea of heaven is apparently a lot different from mine. What are you thinking?'

She put down her fork and looked around the dining room. 'You don't know anything about me apart from what you have picked up through a few Internet searches.'

'That can be changed. And yes, I do know you.'

'Really? You might think you do. Well, I certainly do not know you.'

'Then come to France with me tomorrow and find out for yourself.'

'Thank you, but I have a business to run. What makes you think that I can just take off when I please? Life is not like that.'

'It can be. Let's decide this here and now.'

He grabbed a paper napkin and scribbled something on it and slid it across the table in front of her.

'This is the consultancy fee for your expenses. If, for some crazy reason, you still feel the same way at the end of the week, then Angie will set up the bookings at Elwood House regardless. But if you do decide to buy from me? We will be in the right place at the right time to create something amazing.'

Saskia glared at him for a second and then glanced down at the napkin. And then picked it up and blinked at it in disbelief at a number with lots of zeroes on the end of it.

'You can't be serious,' she gasped.

'You said yourself. Your time is valuable. One week of your time. Seven days. I have a generous marketing budget and every time you serve RB Wines to your prestigious guests at Elwood House you are promoting my company. Your excellent taste. My producers. Take a risk, Saskia. You have nothing to lose. Tempted?'

And, almost casually, he picked up his fork and went back to his pasta.

While she had suddenly lost her appetite.

Unbelievable!

Her gaze landed on the delicious bottle of hugely expensive Italian red wine she was enjoying and she took a long sip to cool her dry throat, taking the time to savour every drop.

Of course she was tempted!

She was running on credit and the nest egg Aunt Margot had left was not going to last much longer. She needed to make Elwood House work. She needed the bookings and she needed them now.

What was she going to do? Ruin her credibility and family reputation for the sake of a few bottles of dodgy wine? Her fingers stilled.

The very last thing she wanted was to get involved with yet another conman who could talk the talk but not deliver the goods and, most importantly, keep his side of the bargain when it came to the push.

Her fingers pressed hard into her forehead as she tried to process everything that Rick had said. And failed.

Oh he was good.

Okay, her father had been a city boy born and bred. Perhaps the similarity ended there. But one thing was abundantly clear. Rick Burgess was every bit the same type of hustler, with the power to make every single woman, and even those not so single, swoon with one look.

Been there. Done that. Still trying to put out the flames.

She was still human, and a girl, but that didn't change a thing.

There was no way she could take this man, who she had only met a few hours earlier, and introduce him as a serious wine merchant to her guests.

How could she even think about putting them through what they had suffered at the hands of her father? He had been credible and his clients adored him.

Hugo Mortimer the man was a delight, the life and soul of any party. Charismatic and charming.

Hugo Mortimer the property developer was a disaster who had destroyed her life and certainly ruined the lives of more than one family around the world who'd trusted their savings to his ridiculous arrogance and high risk schemes.

She just couldn't do it. She couldn't take the risk. Not where Elwood House was concerned.

'I'm not going to France with you, Rick. Don't take it personally. I decided years ago that I wanted to stay independent. That way, there are no compromises or surprises. And I certainly don't want to take orders from someone else once I sign a contract.'

'I understand that.' His smile widened to the point where she thought that she might fall into it and be swallowed up. 'But then I didn't expect you to run Elwood House on your own. The hotel owners I know are notoriously male, egotistical and stubborn. Or at least... That record stood until today. You opened my eyes to what I have been missing.'

His gaze wrapped around her shoulders and neck and slowly, slowly made its way up her face and into her hair, until she had to fight not to squirm under the heat so she frowned at him instead. 'On the other hand, maybe the stubborn bit still applies.'

She leant forwards across the table until her nose was only inches from his.

'I would hate to thwart your expectations. You might never recover from the shock.'

'I think I can handle anything you throw at me,' he replied, his upper lip twitching.

'Really?' Saskia picked up her glass of excellent Italian red and swirled it under her nose before taking a long sip. 'Then come up with a proposal that doesn't involve me selling out my reputation for excellence.'

'Okay. Final offer. If you don't like the wine I offer you then you don't have to buy it. And I still pay your consultancy fee and use Elwood House. Is that any better?'

Saskia tilted her glass until the last drop touched her lips. 'Move your company office into Elwood House. Long-term contract.'

'Done.'

'I can't guarantee that I will buy anything from you. You know that, don't you?'

'Of course. Buy hey, with what I am going to show you, how could you possibly resist? And can I order the Prosecco now?'

She inhaled slowly and then gave a small sharp nod.

And instantly regretted it because he immediately leapt out of his chair, pulled her to her feet by grabbing both shoulders and kissed her hard on the lips. Then he dropped her back down like a sack and rubbed the palms of his hands together.

'Brilliant. What time can you be ready in the morning?'

CHAPTER FIVE

Must-Do list

- *Be sure to pack the spare chargers for phone, camera and notebook computer.*
- *Deliberately leave behind the list of chat-up lines that Kate emailed. Way too dangerous and some of them would crash the car.*
- *Remember your CDs—just in case Rick is a fan of heavy metal.*
- *Stay focused, stay frosty. No getting sidetracked by the lovely view etc. I have a fine view right here in London, thank you.*
- *Try not to worry about the house more than every few minutes. Amber and Kate have things under control. EEP.*

'No, KATE. No more gloves. *Seriously.* I do not need eight pairs of gloves for a week in the French countryside, so please take at least some of them out of my case,' Saskia protested.

'Spoilsport,' Kate hissed and held up a plum-coloured satin slip. 'Amber? What do you think of the seduction power of this one?'

'Not bad, actually,' Amber laughed and sidled over to

Saskia, who was sitting on the bed with her head in her hands.

'Why did I ask you two to help me pack?' Saskia whimpered as Amber gave her a shove. 'I keep telling you. It's a business trip to three vineyards in France—that's all. The Champagne region. Then the Alps and north to Alsace. I am talking muddy fields and icy-cold cellars, not salons fit for satin.'

'A business trip. Yes.' Kate nodded wisely. 'Of course it is.' Then rolled her eyes. 'One week on the road and all alone with the hunk of the year. Believe me, that boy will see you in your lingerie one way or another before the week is out. And you might as well get used to the idea, even if you don't plan to show him your knickers.'

Saskia clutched the edges of her practical thick towelling bath robe tighter across her chest. 'Katherine Lovat!'

Then she sniffed and peered into her suitcase and gave a small shoulder shrug. 'Good thing I only have huge cotton granny pants. They should work as instant boy repellent in case he gets any ideas.'

'That may not be entirely true.' Amber smiled and pulled out a bag from under the bed with the name of an exclusive lingerie shop on the side. 'Kate and I decided that we were being extremely selfish going shopping for fripperies today while you worked, so we splashed out on a little something to brighten your top drawer. I hope you like it.'

'Of course we would have bought a lot more if we had known that you were being wooed by Rick the Reckless, but hey, this should keep him interested and no, you are not allowed to open up your present until the occasion calls for it.'

Saskia smiled and gathered Amber and Kate for a hug on her bed. 'Thanks. I am not going to need it, whatever it is, but you are so kind to me and I promise to wear whatever pretty frilly you have chosen, even if it is to walk up and down freezing-cold wine cellars. I shall feel very special.'

'Of course you will,' Kate snorted. 'But don't forget to book Rick as your date for Amber's wedding. New Year is a busy time for boys and he ticks all the boxes for tall, dark and handsome.'

'My date? This is Rick Burgess you are talking about. He never takes anything seriously. It's as though life is a great joke to be enjoyed at someone else's expense. He's obviously coasting and filling in time before he can slip off to the nearest ski slope or some yacht. Well, I know his type only too well. My dad was exactly the same. Well-off, handsome and super-confident. And a complete disaster when it came to managing his finances and relationships. As far as I'm concerned Rick might as well be standing there waving a red warning sign with the words "Danger. Keep away" written in large black letters.'

Saskia shivered in dramatic horror and then paused and narrowed her eyes as she whizzed around to face Kate. 'Wait a minute. How did you know what he looks like? Oh no. You looked him up on the Internet, didn't you?'

'That was me.' Amber giggled. 'Your Richard is quite the professional sportsman. Very fit. You are a lucky girl.'

'I give up,' Saskia groaned. 'You two are quite incorrigible.'

'That's why you need us,' Kate replied, fluttering her eyelashes. 'And don't worry for a second about this place. Amber is house-sitting and answering the phone and I promise to pop over every evening and gobble up all of the treats in your freezer and drink your wine.'

She paused and waved both arms in the air with a flourish. 'We've got it covered. All you have to do is smile and charm your way through the week with your usual flair. Piece of cake!'

Saskia stood silently on the golden stone patio of the Chateau Morel in the September sunshine and looked out over the rows and rows of neatly trained vines that were destined to create the greatest sparkling wine in the world; champagne.

And thought seriously about dumping Rick and catching the first train back to London.

Piece of cake, Kate had said.

Well, there was nothing sweet about how Saskia would describe the past few hours.

Rick had changed his mind and decided that it would be easier to drive them to the first of the three independent vineyards himself. Which meant that she had been strapped into the passenger seat of the macho four-by-four that Rick had borrowed from one of his team for what had seemed like an eternity.

All the while trapped within arm-touching distance of Rick Burgess on the drive down through the flat countryside of northern France, which she'd thought would never end.

Rick had an incredibly annoying ability to look completely calm and unstressed no matter what delay hit them on the way. The traffic jams on the motorway to the coast—no problem. Dodging in and out of the traffic chaos of the French road works madness as a lorry veered in front of them? It only made him smile that certain smile which turned the corners of his mouth a little higher.

While she was clutching onto the roof straps of the car with both hands in terror.

It was totally infuriating.

The problem was, the more unruffled and calm Rick appeared, the more she wanted to take hold of his shoulders and give him a violent shake and scream out that it was time to wake up and get to work. He could be laid-back any time he wanted, but not now. Not when she had work to do back in London.

Take now, for example. They had been right on schedule arriving in Reims and she was all ready to get started on the details when Rick decided that he needed to take a look at the vines. Leaving her behind in the cellar.

That was two hours ago.

The heels of her high-heeled designer shoes dug into the loose gravel chippings as she tried to walk calmly across the patio and back towards the chateau. She refused to look down and check the damage. Rick would get far too much satisfaction from that. He had taken one look at her footwear that morning and snorted with a dismissive shake of his head. His smart flat leather boots were, of course, perfect for strolling down between the rows of vines and across the rough stone flagstones.

To make matters worse, her cellphone had never stopped ringing from the moment she'd got into Rick's car that morning and, after two hours of terrible mobile reception and her increasing frustration, he had barely given her time to research a few new suppliers of kitchenware before declaring that his car was an Internet-free zone and laptops were not allowed.

She needed to confirm these new bookings for the spring, not make conversation about soil type and climate and all the things that came together to make this small estate unique in over three hundred of the champagne houses in the Reims area of France.

The cheek of the man. She was supposed to be helping

him out! What did he expect her to do? Just forget about Elwood House and treat this trip as some sort of holiday?

Not going to happen.

Even if he was paying her and the setting was absolutely glorious.

The Chateau Morel looked like a white fairy tale castle which had been dropped gently from the sky into the fields of vines.

While the wine? Okay, she had to confess that the champagne that these grapes produced was special. Rare and expensive. In fact, it was precisely the kind of wine that Rick needed to boost the status of his flagship store, after all, there was not a wine shop in the world which did not stock champagne. Elwood Brothers had been famous for their range and quality for decades.

What was even more infuriating was that Rick kept reminding her that she should be excited to see the grapes before harvest! But the truth was she felt too preoccupied and anxious about her work to enjoy the moment.

Saskia rolled her shoulders back with the warm sun on her face as she watched Rick and their host, the Comte de Morel, stroll towards the chateau between the vines, pausing only now and then to taste the grapes. The sound of their gentle chatter rolled towards her.

Just when she thought that he couldn't spring any more surprises on her, Rick had turned the tables. The man she was looking at now was asking exactly the type of intelligent and knowledgeable questions that any grower would expect from another professional.

That was it—professional. Right down to the smart jacket and expensive wristwatch and cufflinks. The denim and boots were just the same. The designer stubble and tousled hair hadn't changed, but his whole attitude and mood had transformed once they'd hit the open road.

If this was Rick trying to impress her and convince her to buy the wine, he was making a fine effort. And, so far, he had not embarrassed her once.

This was not the Rick she had met in London. This was Rick Burgess, the working wine merchant and negotiating charmer. His laughter rang out and suddenly her confidence faltered and she felt out of her depth.

This was so ridiculous.

She was Saskia the calm. Saskia the girl who was always in control. Saskia the girl who knew exactly what she was doing at all times.

It was just that it had been such a long time since she had stepped away from Elwood House and given herself over to someone else to make decisions and take the lead that she was finding it hard to adjust to Rick being in the driving seat.

Excitement combined with anxiety meant that she had barely slept the night before, after the girls had left, with promises to keep them informed on how a little trip with Rick the Reckless, as Kate called him, was going.

If she had come here alone, or with Aunt Margot, she would be able to relax and take the time to learn from the best. Building her knowledge and experience.

But she was way too much on edge to relax for even a second.

Plus, Rick was expecting her to pay attention and make a decision whether to buy this wine, not take time out on holiday. And there was one thing she had learned and promised herself over the years. Once she made a commitment to do something then she would see it through. No false promises. No tricks.

She had promised Rick that she would visit the vineyard and she had. Now came the hard part. Making sure that the Elwood connection was not pulled into whatever Rick was trying to prove here. For better or for worse!

Time to get to work. Because here he was, casually walking towards her as though they had all the time in the world.

'You are looking a bit fierce standing there with your conference folder and pen,' he quipped. 'All ready to stomp into a business meeting and start taking notes.' Then he gestured towards the house. 'I think you scared Pierre off.'

'That is what we are here for, after all. Business. And does the Comte de Morel normally answer to the name Pierre?'

His gaze slid onto her face. By way of her cleavage and neck. Which, of course, made her neck flare up, adding to the embarrassment.

'Why not? That is his name. And I keep telling you, this is the new generation. Pierre prefers guests to be informal.'

Saskia lifted her chin and tugged down on the hem of her smart suit jacket. 'Not sure I can do that. Too many years of training.'

Rick's cellphone rang out with the first beats of a popular dance track and he glanced at a few screens and winced before replying. 'You can put your folder away. Don't worry about the production figures.' He tapped his smartphone with two fingers. 'Pierre has just copied me with the latest costings and projections so we can talk them through when we're back on the road. Now, don't look so surprised. I can do business planning when needed.'

'Surprised?' Saskia cleared her throat, hating that she had been so obvious. 'Not at all, Mr Burgess.'

'It's Rick,' he groaned. 'We are trying to keep things informal. Remember?'

'Is that why you decided to drive yourself?' she asked, teasing him. 'I'm sure that a big company like Burgess

Wine could afford to provide a limo with a driver. Your parents must be pleased that you are taking such interest in the wine business. Quite the entrepreneur, in fact,' she chuckled, looking out over the fields of vines.

'There are okay with it,' he replied, hooking her arm around his elbow and stepping closer so that their bodies were side by side and it was impossible for her to move away. 'Results shout louder than promises. Or something.'

'Okay.' She hesitated, and her feet slowed a little even in the gravel. 'Do they know that we are here today, talking to growers? I don't want to get involved in some family dispute.'

Rick came to a dead stop and whirled around to face Saskia. His gaze locked onto her face. And those grey eyes were suddenly not so warm in the September sunshine, but more like granite. Fierce, commanding but intelligent. For the first time Saskia had a glimpse of some of that inner steel that drove men like Rick to become professional sportsmen. It was the kind of look that had no place in a nice, safe office job.

'Family dispute? What gave you that idea?'

Saskia tensed and licked her lips before replying. 'What I meant to say was that I thought the Burgess Wine empire is based in California. Opening a London branch is a complete departure. It makes me wonder if the company is splitting into separate divisions. That's quite a challenge.'

Rick exhaled slowly then sniffed, as though weighing up what to make of her question.

'Challenge?' Rick's eyebrows crushed together and he frowned. 'Is that what you think?'

But before Saskia could create some sort of answer he tilted his head to one side and gave a small shoulder shrug. 'A challenge,' he repeated, nodding slowly. 'Yeah. When I pitched the idea to my parents last Christmas, they used a few more colourful expressions to describe the notion. A challenge just about sums up the general response.'

'I see,' she replied. 'Wait. Did you say last Christmas? Surely you have seen your parents since then?'

Rick took tighter hold of her hand and started walking towards the house. 'No need. Modern communications. I can work anywhere. They run the business out of Napa and right now the biggest wine festival in the world is about to kick off. They don't want to be involved in the new enterprise in London. Small beer.'

Saskia glanced back at him. She recognised that tiny change in his voice that was so familiar to her it seemed like an old friend. She knew what it was like to defend her parents and their decisions and their over the top lifestyle choices. Especially when those choices did not include her.

What was surprising was that Rick had the same problems she had. Real problems. Problems she recognised only too well. He was trying to keep the tone of his voice light and smiling but below that effortless charm was a well of sorrow.

'You've reminded me that I need to arrange my mother's Christmas present. She's staying in New York with her latest beau this year and I'll be working in London, as always. Thank heavens for telephones.'

He chuckled somewhere deep down in his chest. 'It seems that we have a few parental issues in common.'

'Oh?' she replied in a calm, low voice. 'Is your father in prison too?'

Rick burst out laughing at that and released her hand as he held open the door.

'Touché. You win that one. Why don't we drink champagne and leave our families where they belong? Out of sight and out of our lives. Deal? Deal.'

* * *

'More cheese, Rick? I tried to save you the last slice of the walnut bread but I was too late, Pierre got to it first.'

Anna gestured with the cheese knife towards her husband, Pierre Morel, the tenth generation owner of the Chateau Morel, who threw his hands up into the air in protest. 'Can I help it if I have a healthy appetite? Anyway, you are one to talk. I only turned my back for two minutes to load the dishwasher and what was left of those excellent handmade chocolates Rick brought with him had done a magic disappearing act.'

Anna kissed the top of Pierre's head. 'It's quite true,' she laughed and pressed one very dainty hand to her chest. 'Sweet tooth and a total chocaholic. Now, that is a pretty deadly combination. And I feel totally guilty.'

Rick chuckled and sat back on the wide kitchen chair and patted his stomach. Things had certainly changed an awful lot since he had visited the estate with his parents and Tom as a teenager. The old *comte* and *comtesse* of the Chateau Morel had insisted on serving canapés and coffee in the huge echoing great hall with waiting staff glaring at every crumb which fell onto the thread-bare hand-woven and embroidered carpet. Before the *comte* haughtily declared that he did not sell his prestigious wine to anyone less than premium outlets. He had made it only too clear that the list did not include an online wine retailer who specialised in affordable wine for barbecues and sharing over a plate of pizza.

Now their grandson Pierre and his charming Dutch-born wife Anna were wearing casual trousers and shirts and seemed genuinely delighted to welcome them into their warm, cosy kitchen and a delicious, simple family meal.

'Please don't feel guilty.' Rick smiled. 'It was incredibly kind of you to offer us lunch at such short notice, and I couldn't eat another thing.'

'I could.' Saskia laughed. 'This cheese is amazing.'

'A local goat farmer makes it for us to a traditional recipe. It was one of the first things we stocked in our farm shop and it is always a best seller. I am glad you like it.'

'Delicious,' Saskia replied and cut another wedge. 'And thank you again for the tour. Especially just before harvest. Such an exciting time of year.'

'We have been very lucky with the weather.' Pierre nodded. 'But you're right; this is going to be an excellent vintage.'

'You know, my Aunt Margot always adored Chateau Morel dry champagnes and refused to serve anything else. Although…I do seem to recall that your grandfather persuaded her to try a few magnums of pink champagne for special occasions now and then. It was her special treat on hot summer evenings. Are you planning to continue that tradition?'

Anna shrugged and looked across at Pierre before pouring the coffee. 'We're not sure that there is enough demand to make it worth our while, but it is definitely something we will continue for the next couple of years at least.'

'That's wonderful. I love it so much.'

Pierre nodded and then smiled gently across at Saskia as he rolled his coffee can between his fingers, but when he spoke there was some hesitancy in his voice. 'I remember meeting your Aunt Margot. It must have been about fifteen years or so ago and I was a young apprentice winemaker. I can still remember walking through the doors of Elwood Brothers. Your aunt ran the best wine merchant in London and yet she took the trouble to welcome us as old family friends. She was a remarkable woman and a very

loyal customer. I am only sorry that she never had an opportunity to visit us.'

Anna sat quietly sipping her coffee with her head down
as Pierre squeezed her hand.

'I am sorry too,' Saskia whispered. 'I still miss her very
much. Margot would have adored coming here.'

Saskia pressed the forefingers of her left hand to her
mouth and sucked in a breath and just for a moment looked
as though she was about to start crying.

Rick hadn't expected that!

A trembling flicker of connection started deep in his
stomach. From what Saskia had told him, she was not
close to her mother and he knew that her father was serving time for embezzlement. Her aunt must have been the
only family she could rely on.

Saskia had come here with no clue that she was going
to be emotionally ambushed by a stranger who had known
the aunt she'd so clearly adored.

And now Margot Elwood was gone and she still hadn't
got over it.

Well, he knew what that felt like.

Worse, Saskia was sitting in this kitchen because he
had changed his mind overnight and picked her up in one
of the team's cars and driven them here instead of flying
to Strasbourg and going directly to the *auberge* in Alsace.

His decision. Flying by the seat of his pants. Changing
the rules at the last minute. Stirring things up.

Well, that hadn't worked out so well. He had brought
her here to this place where she was forced to relive her
grief, just when she thought it was all behind her.

Only it was all over her face. Her beautiful, wrecked,
tragic face.

She was feeling that grief and loss all over again.

A familiar pain hit Rick deep inside his heart but he

shoved it down the way he always did when the memory of Tom came flooding back into his consciousness out of the blue. Perhaps it was this chateau? He had such clear memories of that day they had come here as a family.

Now Tom was gone. And he was left to pick up the pieces, just as Saskia was trying to do. *Life wasn't fair. On either of them.*

He shuffled in his chair and picked up another slice of cheese and bread and casually looked up with a wave of his cheese knife.

Rick chuckled out loud, instantly cutting through the tense atmosphere.

'That's why I'm working so hard to bring your champagne to customers like Saskia. The girl right here today has inherited the best qualities of the Elwood family and her clients expect the very best. Which is precisely what we are going to give them. Saskia and I are looking forward. Not backward. Aren't you?'

A faint glimmer of a smile flickered across Pierre's face and Anna's expression lightened.

'I could not have put it better myself, Rick. Of course, that was a different generation and that is exactly what we want to do; move forward.'

'Why else am I here?' Rick smiled and relaxed back in his chair. 'And thank you for being so honest and generous, and for your time today so close to the harvest. Don't forget, next time you're in London I'll be delighted to return your hospitality and show you around our new showroom. In the meantime?' He raised his coffee cup. 'I think a toast is required. To a successful harvest and many of them!'

'Well,' Rick said with a low sigh, 'that went well. Nice lunch. What did you think of the extra dry champagne? That is a winner in my book.'

'A winner? Yes, the champagne was lovely and I will definitely order some. Out of guilt if nothing else,' Saskia said in a voice that was trembling with emotion. 'That lovely couple gave us such a warm welcome and all I could do was fall apart. They must think that I am a complete idiot.'

She half turned towards him in the passenger seat and grabbed hold of the dashboard to give her strength. 'I cannot believe that I embarrassed myself like that. I had no idea that Pierre had met Aunt Margot and admired her, but I certainly don't normally react that way. I suppose it hit me out of the blue, but it was still so humiliating.'

'Who for? Me?' Rick glanced once at Saskia before concentrating on driving down the narrow farm road. 'Not at all. What is there to be embarrassed about? You cared for your aunt and she was clearly admired.'

His fingers tapped out a rhythm on the steering wheel. 'How long has it been?'

'Just over a year.' Saskia exhaled slowly and when she spoke her words were very calm and measured. 'But it feels a lot longer.'

Rick said nothing but slowed the car on the narrow country road and pulled into the next tourist viewpoint on the brow of a hill.

Before Saskia knew what was happening, he was out of the car and had opened the passenger door for her.

'Come on,' he said, and held out his hand towards her. 'Let's get some air.'

'Air?' she repeated disbelievingly. 'I have had more than enough air at the Chateau, thank you. I can be just as miserable right here.'

'Then have some more. I'm not driving another mile until we have this out.'

He stood there, looking at her with a smile on his face

which reached his eyes and was impossible to resist. His fingers twitched, gesturing her to reach out and take his hand.

Resigned to the inevitable and too exhausted to complain further, Saskia slowly and carefully unclipped her seat belt, took his hand and stepped down onto the grass in her smart heels.

But, instead of releasing her hand, Rick wrapped his fingers firmly around hers and drew her away from the car and onto the brow of the hill, where they stood in silence looking out onto the golden leaves and autumn colours of the neat rows of grapevines. Side by side. So that when he broke the silence it was as if he was talking to the vines.

Rick rolled his shoulders. 'I know what it is like to lose someone you love. And believe me when I say that a year is not nearly long enough to get over wanting to burst into tears just at the sound of that person's name. But nobody in the world will think less of you if you miss your aunt. Nobody.'

Then he sniffed and gazed out at the golden autumn colours.

'Do you know what I'm thinking?' For several long minutes all Saskia could hear was the *tink, tink, tink* from the car as it cooled and birdsong from the fields stretched out in front of them.

'That inside my business suit I'm a fraud?' she whispered.

He whipped around towards her and his blue-grey eyes turned into the colour of steel as they glared at her. Hard, demanding and not prepared to take any argument.

'Wrong. And don't you ever let anyone make you feel that way. Ever. You are not a fraud. Okay, so you get emotional and blub over your silk blouse. Only to be expected. Just think how hard it is for us guys! We have to play the macho game and wait until we get home to let rip. So get that out of your head right now, gorgeous. Not a fraud. Are we clear?'

'Okay.' She blinked and drew back a little. 'Quite clear.'

'Good. I don't want to hear it again. You are, however, the worst mind-reader I've ever met. Because actually—' and his voice lowered and seemed to warm in the sunshine '—I was thinking about how very lucky we are.'

He flung his right hand out towards the hills and his left hand clung on to Saskia even more tightly as though he was afraid she might run away.

'Look at this view. The birds are singing and the sun is shining. No traffic noise. No buses, taxis, or email or a clamour of people demanding our attention. For the next few minutes this is all ours. And I happen to think it's special.'

He turned back to her with a smile, reached out and stroked her cheek with one finger so tenderly and gently, and she felt like crying for real. 'Change of plan. I was thinking of staying overnight at this great hotel some friends of mine own, but you know what? It's time to go home. No. Not London, the chalet in the French Alps that I call home. I've done enough talking. Time for action. That way, we can take time out to enjoy ourselves tomorrow morning before the wedding.'

'Wedding? What wedding?' Saskia asked.

'You'll see.' Rick laughed and tapped the end of her nose with his finger. 'You'll see.'

CHAPTER SIX

Must-Do list
- *Be sure to buy Alpine red and white fabric to make Christmas soft furnishings and decorations. Take photos of the window displays for ideas.*
- *The wine and cuisine from this part of France is very interesting and delicious. Pick up some recipe books and ideas.*
- *Never forget that Rick is a salesman and try not to weaken in this gorgeous chalet with its amazing views.*

'I CAN'T BEGIN to describe how gorgeous this chalet is,' Saskia whispered with a long sigh. 'Think tourist postcards of the Alps. All golden wood and snow-capped mountain views with ancient wooden skis stacked in the hall. And window boxes. Rick has window boxes with real red balcony geraniums hanging out of them. I didn't expect that.'

Just like I didn't expect him to back me up yesterday after the Chateau Morel.

'The fiend,' Kate sniffed, and Saskia could tell that her friend had the phone jammed in the corner between her chin and her shoulder. 'Log cabins and mountain views? I think you should call the authorities immediately. The next thing you know, he will be opening doors for you and helping you on with your coat. I can see it now. All part of his ruthless plan to lower your resistance and make you like him!'

'Well, it's working. Coat. Tick. Doors. Tick. He even brought my suitcase inside and insisted on taking me out to dinner last night. Which was amazing. I had no idea that Savoyard food was so delicious. And of course he knows everyone. So they immediately thought that I was, and I quote—"his new squeeze". Hah! As if.'

'You tell them,' Kate replied. 'Your standards are much higher. Sort of. Well, they would be if you ever actually dated, but you know what I mean. Higher. Who wants a tall, dark and handsome hunk on her arm anyhow? Oh no. Or should that be yes?'

'Well, thanks. You are a lot of help.'

'You don't need help. You have never needed help,' Kate laughed. 'So, just for once, go with the flow and see where it takes you! How about that for an idea? Oh—must go. My client has arrived and this jacket is still missing a pocket. Bye!'

'Bye,' Saskia replied, but Kate had already gone. Busy as always. Which was great. Kate had worked hard to make her fashion design business a success. But it didn't stop her from worrying about Elwood House, no matter how wonderful the diversion.

Saskia sat back in her comfy bedroom chair and stared out of the square wooden window at the stunning view of Mont Blanc set against a bright blue sky. It was so perfect that it could have been a framed photograph instead of a real, huge, snow-covered mountain.

When they'd driven into Chamonix the previous evening the sun was starting to set behind Mont Blanc and the whole peak and the glacier that streamed down into their valley had been touched with a strange pink glow which she had never seen before. It was almost as if the mountains were blushing.

Well, she knew all about that. She hadn't been joking about the good-natured teasing Rick had received from the locals and restaurant staff about his new lady friend—her! Introducing her as a business colleague had made them laugh even louder. If she picked up the accent correctly, it was very rare for Rick to bring anyone but fellow professional sportsmen to his chalet, and never a woman, so she was a definite first.

In Chamonix, Rick was very much a man's man.

Perhaps that was why he was so keen to say goodnight as soon as they'd got back to the chalet?

Not that she was complaining. Far from it. She had been treated to a delicious meal with local wine and was feeling a lot mellower when she walked through the door into the warm and cosy log cabin.

It simply would have been nice to talk about his plans for his programme of vineyard visits without an audience within earshot of everything that they were saying. She had so many questions. And so few answers.

Starting with the wedding she had been invited to today.

It was a lovely idea, but they didn't have time to go to his friends' wedding. She needed to get back to work on her plans for Elwood House and go through the vineyard production forecasts Rick had promised he would provide, rather than wedding plans. But he had refused to take no for an answer.

All Rick would say was that it was one of the ten couples whose wine they would be selling, and that was it! No details at all.

Rick Burgess seriously needed to work on his communication skills.

Time to help him with that. Starting right now!

Saskia stood up and checked her side and front view in the mirror. The wedding was not until that afternoon so she could be smart casual for a few hours. Fitted three-quarter length black trousers and black medium heels. High-neck ivory silk shirt. Hair sleeked back. Discreet make-up. Simple jewellery. Yes. That would do for any impromptu business meetings he might have set up to surprise her.

Because, one way or another, she needed to get this business trip back on track and focused on the work. Even if she was enjoying herself far more than she was prepared to admit.

She lifted her chin and saluted her reflection with a grin. All present and correct. Ready to face the world.

She marched over and flung open the bedroom door. And stood there. Frozen.

Because Rick was standing next to the dining room table, surrounded by what looked to her like the entire contents of a camping store. With extras. He was wearing black ski wear which clung to the bands of muscles across his chest and abdomen. And hot did not come close to describing how fit he looked.

'Dare I ask?' she muttered.

He looked up and smiled in a totally casual and relaxed fashion. 'Morning. Hope you slept well.'

'Very well, thank you. And please explain.'

He gestured with his head towards the table. 'Help yourself to breakfast and I'll do my best. We're setting off in about an hour.'

Saskia made her way carefully across the floor by standing on tiptoe to avoid treading on the equipment. Laid on the table was a wonderful platter of continental cooked meats, cheese and Danish pastries and croissants. Fresh butter and jams. Fruit. 'You must have been up early.

But why are you dressed like that? I thought we had a business meeting today and an hour doesn't seem long enough.'

Rick nodded and adjusted something which had the word 'Altimeter' on the side before setting it down next to his plate. 'Small town. Baker and supermarket are right next to each other. Makes it easy.'

He pointed with the end of a hand-held radio to a ceramic pot covered with a red and white checked fabric circle. 'Try the wild blueberry jam. My neighbour collected the berries this week high on the mountain; it's pretty good. And relax, I haven't forgotten what we are here for.'

Saskia sat down and broke up a croissant and piled it with the jam. He was right, it was amazing. Almost as good as the view of her host, who was standing right in front of a large glass-panelled door which led out onto a wooden veranda. There was a perfect backdrop of green forest, blue sky and the snow-white mountain Mont Blanc behind his head and a professional stylist could not have created a better composition in a million years.

And, just like that, something flipped deep inside Saskia's stomach and she slowed down to appreciate every mouthful of her breakfast, and every eyeful.

Rick really was spectacular.

Also a mind-reader because, just as she was ogling his chest, Rick glanced around at her and caught her in the act and grinned that knowing kind of grin which made it ten times worse. Saskia knew that her neck was flaming red as she blushed, especially wearing a pale shirt, but there was nothing she could do about it. So she loaded up her plate from the platter instead.

'You were about to tell me where we are off to,' she said in a calm, controlled voice, knowing all the while that it wasn't fooling him in the slightest.

'A treat for you.' He smiled and strolled over with a pot

of the most delicious-smelling coffee and poured her a cup. 'After weeks on the road, I needed to step away from the business and get back to my life. But today? Today, I think it's time for you to meet one of our ten growers.'

'Good idea.' She nodded. 'Is the vineyard very far? I need ten minutes to charge my laptop and camera and I'll be ready to take minutes.'

'Just in the next valley, but that's not where we're going. Oh no. Jean Baptiste has a passion for flying as well as grapes. Time to show you just how much fun you can have if you team up with me.'

The buttered slice of baguette halted halfway to her lips. 'Flying?' she whimpered.

'Of course. We. Are going paragliding. Saskia? Are you okay? You are looking a little pale.'

She just managed to put her breakfast down without dropping it.

'*Paragliding,*' she whispered, feeling that her throat was full of breadcrumbs.

'Sure,' Rick replied, stuffing all kinds of helmets and equipment into a huge backpack. 'Burgess Wine sponsors the local paragliding club and I won a few championships a couple of years ago and like to keep up the practice. Have you ever tried it yourself?'

Saskia blinked at him and tried to form a sensible reply but gave up. 'Is that where you tie a parachute to your back and jump off a cliff and hope the chute slows you down before you hit the ground?'

'Not quite, but you have the general idea about controlling the descent with a canopy.'

She inhaled slowly and decided to break the bad news all at once.

'I am really sorry, especially since you stuck your neck out for me yesterday, but I have vertigo on a stepladder and have to pay people to climb up and clean my bedroom windows because I can't lean out and do it myself.'

She shook her head slowly from side to side. 'I don't do heights.'

His hands stilled and he looked at her, eyebrows high. 'Seriously?'

'Seriously.' She nodded very slowly, up and down. Twice.

'Oh—' he sniffed '—not a problem. You can jump onto my harness and I can fly you down in tandem. I do it all the time and you don't weigh a thing. Wait and see, you'll enjoy it. But er...' His gaze scanned her from head to toe and then back up again and there was just enough of a cheeky grin on his face to make her want to cover her chest with a cushion. 'You might want to change your clothes. Have you brought any ski wear?'

She narrowed her eyes and tilted her head slightly to one side before replying. 'Strange. As a matter of fact, I have not. You see, I packed for a business trip. Fancy that!'

An hour later, Saskia had changed into cold weather layers, survived being driven by Rick to a ski lift at breakneck speed and then a hair-raising trip trapped inside a glass-sided gondola which took twenty minutes to climb up the side of the valley wall.

The good news was that Rick had kept her talking and focused on him for the whole journey and she had not lost her breakfast as the gondola slid up the loose cable, juddering along every pole before coming to a gentle swaying halt at the top.

It was almost worth it for the views. Stepping out from the ski station, Saskia was hit square between the eyes by a panorama of the snow-covered mountains on each side of the valley that was so breathtakingly lovely that she for-

got that she was supposed to be scared for all of five minutes—before she turned around and saw Rick talking to
another man carrying another huge backpack.

'Saskia, come and meet Jean Baptiste Fayel. Jean is
one of my winemakers I was telling you about who we
are going to showcase in the London store.'

A handsome fair-haired young man stepped forward. If
Saskia thought that Rick had a firm handshake then Jean
Baptiste was trying to do a fine job of shaking her arm
out of its socket.

'Great to meet you, Miss Elwood.' He grinned, still
shaking her hand. 'Rick has told us all about the fantastic
plans you have to serve our wine. We're really excited.'

'Leave the poor girl alone.' Rick laughed and shook Jean
by the shoulders before turning to Saskia. 'Jean is getting
married this afternoon so we thought that it would do us
good to escape away from the mayhem back at his house
and get into the air for a few hours.'

This was the bridegroom?

Saskia turned back to Jean with a smile. 'Congratulations. How wonderful.'

He blushed slightly, which was very charming. 'Thank
you, and of course you're invited to the wedding. Nicole
and I would love to see you there. Rick has given us a
lifeline to a great opportunity. And that is something to
celebrate.'

Saskia flashed a glance at Rick, who nodded slowly.

*She had been ambushed! Any chance of doing work was
now completely out of the window!*

'I'm looking forward to it,' Saskia replied with a smile.
'Thank you.'

'Excellent,' he replied and then nodded towards the cliff
and checked his chronometer. 'If you'll excuse me, my future bride has a house full of guests who cannot start the

eating and drinking until I get back. See you at the landing strip. But you go first. I'll follow on.'

Rick came up and stood next to Saskia and they watched Jean Baptiste stroll casually over to the edge of the cliff, sit down as though there was not a huge drop only feet in front of him and unpack the same type of huge sack that Rick had brought.

It was like a magical toy box with an invisible bottom. Helmets, ropes, gloves and clothing, instruments like the ones she had seen in the kitchen that morning and then finally a tightly folded huge blue and red piece of canopy fabric emerged from one single bag. It was unbelievable! And scary.

She was still watching him slip into a harness when Rick slid closer and whispered into her ear. 'You've just been talking to one of the most promising members of the French paragliding team. Jean Baptiste is a star. All I can do is help him with a few pointers now and then when he thinks he needs coaching. But he knows what he is doing.'

'Good,' Saskia gasped. 'Because I am terrified just watching him walk over the edge onto that slope. I have no idea how he can do that.'

Rick burst out laughing and she scowled at him.

'It's not funny. We all have our weaknesses and this happens to be mine,' she whispered through clenched teeth. 'And you really should warn me about these little adventures in advance. You knew that I wouldn't be able to refuse Jean Baptiste and I have so much work to do I'm never going to catch up.'

'Where would be the fun in that? So you're not tempted to take up my offer and jump into the harness with me?' he asked, waggling his eyebrows up and down several times, and then reared back. 'Oh, now that is a fierce look. I'll take it as a no.'

Rick pressed a hand to the small of her back and guided her just a little closer to the edge, then opened her hand, splayed out her fingers and flashed her one of his killer smiles. For just one second Saskia thought that he might kiss her fingers, but instead he dropped a large bunch of keys onto her palm and closed her fingers over them.

'I'm flying down. But I could really use a pickup from the landing site. You can work out where it is. Please try not to crash my truck, and have some fun! I'm going to.'

Fun! Crash!

Saskia glared at the keys but when she looked up Rick was already sitting just below Jean Baptiste on the slope, on the steep curvature of the mountain with his backpack open, splaying out the ropes of his parachute and equipment.

Risking vertigo, Saskia edged closer to the cliff so that she could see what he was doing. 'Do be careful,' she called out. He must've heard her because he replied with a quick salute to his helmet and then untangled one of the ropes which ran between his harness and the bright orange curve of a fluted canopy which extended behind his head.

Then, as she watched with her hand pressed over her mouth, her hair whipping in front of her face in the breeze, Rick got to his feet. He took a couple of steps forward and the canopy seemed to inflate all on its own behind him, making the rope lines go straight.

And then Rick Burgess ran off the edge of the mountain.

Her heart leapt into her throat. She could not move. Dared not move. But, by leaning one more inch closer to the edge, she could see that his parachute had formed a perfect rippling rainbow arc in the sky just below her. She couldn't move her gaze from the tiny figure suspended by the ropes below.

He was sitting in some form of fabric seat made from

his harness, with his legs dangling over... Nothing but air. Hundreds of feet, possibly thousands of feet, of air.

Saskia sucked in a breath as the orange canopy fluttered slightly as he turned it towards the forest of pine trees they had passed over on the way up from the safety of the gondola ski lift.

He was spinning out of control and was going to crash into the forest! Saskia's hand pressed firmly into her mouth. But he didn't. The parachute made a slow, gentle spiral away from the rocky mountainside and forests below and turned back across the valley, spiralling in slow wide circles ever downward.

Her hands were clutching the keys so hard as she watched him descend that the points were pressing painfully into her flesh, but she could not look away. She had to keep watching Rick as he circled down, down, moving towards the mountain and then back towards the Chamonix valley. Their landing field was so far below the viewpoint that for a fraction of a second she lost sight of Rick behind some trees on the ground.

Had his harness come undone? Had he fallen out? No. She was able to breathe again. There he was. Moving in tighter and tighter circles towards the other parachute. And just when she thought he was on the same height as the first trees next to the white flowing river, he was down. On the ground. Safe.

Saskia's legs gave way and she sat down heavily on the rough path of gravel and Alpine grasses.

Collapsed down would be a better description.

Now she could breathe again. *If she remembered how. Because Jean Baptiste was getting ready to do exactly the same thing! And he was getting married today!*

Her chest had only risen and fallen a few times when the familiar ringtone of her cellphone sang out and she flicked it open to read a text message: *Down safe and well. Great flight. See you soon. R.*

Her fingers clumsily stabbed at the keypad. *Terrifying. Heading back now. S.*

Her shoulders slumped. And she flicked her phone closed.

Rick had been impressive. Watching his flight had been terrifying, horrific, awe-inspiring—and totally exhilarating at the same time.

Rick clearly did know what he was doing and Jean Baptiste respected him as a friend and a mentor and as a coach. That meant a lot.

The two men were friends and sportsmen working together to make something remarkable happen. A tiny bubble of pride in what Rick had achieved rose up from her admiration and popped into her brain before her logic could burst it.

How many more sides to Rick Burgess were there?

She had seen Rick in full-on salesman mode at Elwood House back in London.

Rick the wine merchant was a different man at the Chateau Morel and now Rick the friend and paraglider was taking the lead at home in the Alps.

She had never met anyone who was so capable of astonishing her on a daily basis.

His life seemed to be one series of constant personal challenges, all fuelled by a burning sense of life and energy and passion and drive.

No doubt about it. He was an achiever and he worked hard for those achievements.

Kate had been wrong about him.

He was not Rick the Reckless. He knew the risks and made the judgement call based on skills and talent and experience rather than some arrogant sense of his own self-importance.

Perhaps she was wrong about the wine store? Perhaps this was not a vanity project, but a real business initiative created by someone with genuine entrepreneurial zeal and passion for what they believed in.

Saskia stood up and brushed the dirt from the seat of her pants, then looked over the cliff for the landing site far below, where a blue canopy was now stretched out next to an orange one and she instantly felt sick and dizzy.

She might have been wrong about Rick, but there was one thing she was definitely clear about. There was no way she would ever, *ever,* jump off a cliff with a fabric bag above her head to break her fall. Even if she was strapped to Rick at the time.

She liked her feet to stay firmly on solid ground. Safe.

She stepped back from the edge and started strolling down to the ski station to catch the gondola back to the valley.

A cold hollow feeling swelled up in the pit of her stomach and it had nothing to do with the icy-cold wind that was blowing in from the snowy peaks around her.

She recognised that feeling only too well. It was a present from her old friends, fear and anxiety.

What was she doing here?

There was only one way this trip was going to end and it was in disappointment and regret for both of them.

She was too afraid to make the leap.

Whether that was running off a mountain strapped to Rick, or taking such risks in her life.

She dared not risk that precious security that she had worked so hard to create by giving her time and energy to RB Wines, and it would be a lot of her time, she could see that now.

Now all she had to do was work out how to tell Rick that she could not accept what he had to offer; and mean it.

CHAPTER SEVEN

Must-Do list
- *You are going to a wedding—the worst kind of emotional blackmail. Rick should be ashamed.*
- *It is okay to admit that you are not keen on heights. This is not a weakness at all. Simply a statement of fact.*
- *It is okay to admire men who jump off mountains with a grin on their face—just for fun. But that does not mean that you have to buy wine from them. Oh no.*
- *It is okay to let people surprise you on a daily basis.*

'WHAT A LOVELY dress. That colour is amazing on you.'

'Thank you, kind sir,' Saskia replied and turned around to face Rick. 'My friends tell me that coral is very fashionable this season and...' But then the words stuck in her throat.

Rick Burgess was wearing a suit. And not just any suit. This was a silk and cashmere blend that Kate would have slobbered over. Midnight-blue with a tiny paler blue stripe, which fitted his broad shoulders and narrow waist to perfection.

Matched with a pale blue shirt which highlighted his tan and a pink and blue tie.

He looked like a male model who had just walked off a fashion display. Tall, dark, clean-shaven, swept back hair and so handsome it was a joke. There were movie actors who did not look that good.

'My, this is quite a transformation, Mr Burgess.'

Rick glanced down at his suit and smiled. 'Oh this little old thing? I like to wear it now and again to keep the moths away.'

'Moths? Um. So you wear a gorgeous made-to-measure suit, and yes, I know that to be a fact because my very good friend Kate is a fashion designer, for a local wedding in rural France, but choose a leather jacket for a business meeting in London? How curious. You really do like to play with people's expectations, don't you?'

'Play? Are you implying that this is some sort of a game, Miss Elwood?'

Saskia strolled forward on her high heeled sandals and reached up and straightened out the yellow rosebud on his lapel and then stepped back, gave his jacket one final pat and nodded.

'Maybe. But you are quite an expert player. I have tried so many times over the past few days to switch to work or our business and so far you have succeeded in diverting me to a fabulous champagne chateau, a paragliding flight and now a wedding party. I can squeeze in two hours tops but that is it! Seriously! Should I expect fireworks and a grand finale before we actually get around to doing the work?'

He snorted out loud and strolled over to the fireplace, which was crackling with resin from the pine wood logs, and picked up a set of cufflinks from the mantelpiece.

'You're starting to understand. I do things my way. We'll get the work done. You wait and see.'

Saskia sighed and picked up a silver-framed photograph from the bookshelf next to the fireplace. In the photograph, Rick was standing on what looked like a podium, dressed in black ski shirt and trousers and mirror shades, with his arm around a taller man who was squinting at the camera as the sun reflected back from the snow. The taller man was wearing smart beige trousers with a crisp front pleat and a formal check shirt and tie. In contrast to Rick, his body language was stiff and he looked very uncomfortable standing on the snow.

She sensed rather than heard that Rick had strolled closer and looked over her shoulder at him.

'Is this your brother? Tom, isn't it?'

Rick glanced at the photograph in her hands, then coughed out loud. 'That's Tom all right. *Not* one of life's natural sportsmen. He turned up out of the blue just in time to see me take the championship for jumping from the top of Mont Blanc. Typical. Right place and right time. I think it was the first time he had ever been on a mountain in the snow and I seem to remember that he had a problem with the ski lift.'

Rick glanced at Saskia and smiled. 'In those days it was a wooden bench attached to a chain bar at the front to stop you from falling out, but your legs dangled over the huge drop.' He shook his head. 'We came down off the mountain in a snow plough. Can you believe that?'

'That sounds perfectly sensible. I understand completely.' She laughed and replaced the picture on the shelf. 'I would have done exactly the same thing. What is Tom doing now? Is he still in the wine trade?'

Rick's eyebrows came together and he turned away from her and slowly walked over to the fireplace and rested one hand on the mantelpiece as he raked over the burning logs with a heavy metal poker.

Rick?

His gaze was locked onto the burning embers, but when he replied his voice was ice-cold. 'I thought that you already knew. Tom died, Saskia. He died two years ago.'

She gasped and crossed the gap between them and laid her hand gently on his arm.

He looked around and their eyes locked for a few seconds before a silent smile clicked back on.

And in that instant her heart melted.

Because, for the first time since they'd met, she knew that she had finally seen the real Richard Burgess beneath the tough man shell.

He had lost the brother he adored and it still hurt. It hurt so badly that he was incapable of expressing it. Two years was not nearly long enough to recover from that kind of loss.

Two years. Why did that stick in her mind?

Of course. Rick had been working for Burgess Wine for two years.

She should have known. She should have done her research.

Saskia broke the silence, her voice low, to disguise her thumping heart. 'I am so sorry. I didn't mean to pry. It was really none of my business and I feel awful to have brought back such painful memories.'

Rick answered by reaching out and taking Saskia's hand in his, startling her. He slowly splayed out each finger as she tried to clench her hand into a fist and stared down at her palm.

She couldn't breathe. Could hardly dare to speak at the sadness and regret in the man's voice; a sadness that almost overwhelmed her, a sadness that made her want to wrap her arms around him and hold him.

'Long life line.' He looked up into her eyes. 'Most people take a little longer to make the connection, but you've worked it out already, haven't you?'

He lifted one hand and pushed his hair back from his forehead. 'No regrets. Once an adrenalin junkie, always an adrenalin junkie. But you know what? We were not so different. Tom used to get exactly the same rush from solving some complex IT problem. He loved his work. Couldn't get enough.'

Saskia looked up and raised her eyebrows, and let him continue.

Rick stopped and physically turned Saskia around and gestured towards the window, which was dominated by the towering mountain that was Mont Blanc.

'I remember when that photograph was taken as though it was yesterday. The biting cold. The brilliant sunshine. The exhilaration that comes from jumping from the top of the mountain with only a parachute and a pair of skis!'

He looked at Saskia and grinned. 'Those sorts of memories have to be earned. You can't buy them or trade them. You just have to be there, at that moment in time and space. That's special. And Tom understood that. He really did. He had built up Burgess Wine from nothing by risking the business on an Internet system for selling wine which he didn't know would work or not. We were both risk-takers, just in different fields. We had so many great ideas about working together on some grandiose project or other, but not once did he ever try and make me walk away from life as a sportsman. That was always going to have to be my choice.'

Saskia turned her back on Rick, then whipped around, her voice trembling. 'I've never understood it. Never. People in London who knew my parents think that I have somehow come to terms with the terrible risks my dad took with other people's money for years before it all collapsed, but they are so wrong. You heard it with your own ears at Chateau Morel. People have long memories. They remember your brother for the best reasons and my dad for the worst. And, like it or not, we are both suffering from the fallout.'

She stretched out her hand towards Rick as he started to speak, but she turned back to face him so quickly that he caught her off balance, and he had to grab her around the waist and pull her towards him to steady her.

Saskia pushed down on his shoulders to steady herself, and made the mistake of looking into his face. And was lost, drowning in the deep pools of his eyes, which seemed to magically bind her so tight that resistance was futile. She tried to focus on the tanned, creased forehead above a mouth that was soft and wide.

Lush.

He was wearing an aftershave that smelt of warm spice, his head and throat were only inches from her face, her bosom pressed against the fine fabric. In a fraction of a second, Saskia was conscious that his hand had taken a firmer grip around her waist, moving over her thin silk dress as though it was the finest lingerie, so that she could sense the heat of his fingertips on her warm skin beneath.

She felt something connect in her gut, took a deep breath and watched words form in that amazing mouth.

'I think we make our own destiny...' Rick whispered, his gaze locked onto her eyes, and slowly closed the gap between their bodies, drawing her towards him by invisible ropes of steel.

'Destiny...?' she whispered.

'Who dares wins. Don't you take chances, Saskia?'

'Only with you...' Saskia replied, but the words were driven from her mind as Rick's fingers wound up into her hair and, drawing her closer, he slanted his head so that his warm, soft lips gently glided over hers, then firmer, hotter.

The sensation blew away any vague idea that might have been forming in her head that she could resist this man for one second longer. Her eyes closed as heat rushed from her toes to the tips of her ears and everything else in the world was lost in the giddy sensation.

She wanted the earth to stop spinning so that this moment could last for ever.

Before she could change her mind, Saskia Elwood closed her eyes and kissed Rick Burgess back, tasting the heat of his mouth, a heady smell of coffee, chocolate crumbs and aftershave, sensing his resistance melt as he moved deeper into the kiss, her own arms lifting to wrap around his neck.

She let the pressure of his lips and the scent and sensation of his body warm every cell in her body before she finally pulled her head back.

Rick looked up at her with those blue-grey eyes, his chest responding to his faster breathing, and whispered, 'Here's to taking chances,' before sliding his hand down the whole length of her back and onto her waist, the pressure drawing her forward as he moved his head into her neck and throat, kissing her on the collarbone, then up behind her ears, his fingers moving in wide circles over her back.

'Hey Rick, just to let you know that I dropped that champagne off at Nicole's place... Oops. Later...'

Saskia opened her eyes in time to see the back of a man's coat jog out of the door and in one single movement she pulled back and smoothed down the ruffled fabric of her dress with one hand as she gathered up her hair, which had mysteriously become untied.

'I...er...need to get my bag,' Saskia just about managed

to stammer out and waved her hand towards the bedroom. 'Handbag. For the wedding. And do something with my hair. Ten minutes.'

Rick coughed. 'Great idea. Ten minutes. Right.'

Rick stood at the table and flicked through his notes on the speech that he planned to give at the wedding party, but the words refused to sink in.

All he could think about was Saskia.

He hadn't planned to kiss her or touch her but one touch was all it needed for him to give in to the magnetic attraction he'd felt for Saskia since that first time he'd seen her standing on the pavement only a few days earlier.

His eyes squeezed tight with frustration.

When had he become such an idiot? And just when he'd thought that she was close to agreeing to work with him, trying to achieve something. Together. As his business partner and best customer, not his lover.

He had tried that before with a girl he'd thought he knew and been burnt.

Saskia had been honest with him from day one.

She was scared about stepping outside her world and working with him, he could see that. And now he might just have blown their fledgling relationship out of the water.

In a few short days Saskia had become a friend, the person he wanted to talk to and spend time with.

But what happened now?

Because one thing was clear. He would only make a commitment to Saskia Elwood that he was prepared to deliver. His life could change at a moment's notice. He was the last kind of man who could give her what she needed.

Last night in the restaurant his neighbours had teased him mercilessly with their gentle ribbing about him bringing a girl home for once. Even the waitress had whispered sweet words about his pretty *'amour'* in his ear on the way out. And now he was off to Nicole and Jean's wedding with an unexpected lady guest.

Little wonder that his friend had seen him with Saskia and thought they were more than work colleagues.

Well, they were wrong. *In so many ways.* He was not the kind of man who wanted a long-term relationship and Saskia must have worked that out for herself. She was a clever girl.

Except…when he'd kissed her face? Everything had changed.

No going back. But maybe, just maybe, he could rescue their friendship and build on it. Create a bond that was more than physical. A bond that linked them through a common passion for the one thing they both knew about. Family.

She would know not to expect anything more from him, wouldn't she?

CHAPTER EIGHT

Must-Do list
- *Be sure to take lots of photos of the outdoor wedding theme. Would it work in a walled garden and patio in London?*
- *Focus on the cake and the food and lighting. Take notes and cadge a few recipes if you can from the locals.*
- *Remember to take tissues in case you embarrass yourself at the wedding.*
- *Do NOT let Rick talk you into buying their entire wine production as a wedding present, no matter how much you would like to. BAD idea. Taste it first and check the numbers. Heart. Head. Frosty*

'Hey. This is a wedding. You are not supposed to be in the kitchen,' Rick whispered into her ear as he sauntered up to her and grabbed her around the middle. 'Although I suppose it is an improvement on taking notes on your smartphone during your tour of the cellars.'

'Who, me?' Saskia answered, both of her hands too occupied at that moment to fend him off or scold him. 'I have officially given up all hope of doing anything work-wise for the next few hours so I am forced to enjoy myself. And the bride needs to be with her family, not plating up choux buns. I am happy to help out since they were kind enough to invite me.'

'Agreed. It's been years since I've seen a proper champagne sword being put to such excellent use in demolishing a toffee profiterole tower. And they say chivalry is dead.'

'It was the highlight of the cake-cutting ceremony.' Saskia nodded. 'Nicole's mother made the croquembouche fresh this morning, with lots of help from her two nephews. They are the eight and six-year-olds who are running around on the table right now, high on fat and sugar. Apparently they gobbled up any odd-looking profiteroles so they wouldn't spoil the display. It was very generous of them.'

'Family loyalty. And you can't beat a proper profiterole tower for impact.'

'Quite right. In fact, this gives me an idea for the perfect wedding cake for my friend Amber, who's getting married at Elwood House at New Year. I'm thinking golden profiteroles, crème patissèrie, toffee sauce and a cloud of caramel veil, but with fresh mango and raspberry. Delicious! Orchids on the side.'

Rick picked up one of the choux buns with his fingers and bit into it. Saskia simply shook her head and carried on plating out the delicate pastries, using two spoons to break up the crystal caramel and dividing the profiteroles into groups of four on lovely china plates.

'Pretty good,' he murmured and popped the other half into his mouth. 'And I don't have a sweet tooth.'

'Excellent. More for the rest of us.' She laughed and slid the plates onto the dessert table, where they were whisked away, with the platters of mini macaroons and tiny light-as-a-feather fairy cakes topped with fresh berries, to the round tables which filled the patio around the central fountain outside the main stone house where the wedding had been held. 'Because I do have a sweet tooth and this is heaven.'

Rick wiped his hands down and peered at what was left of the tower as she cracked through the crisp caramel and divided out the buns. 'I would say at a guess that you've done that before.'

Saskia stood back and admired the table. 'I now declare that this croquembouche is officially demolished. And yes, I have broken up caramel shards and clouds before.'

'Well, in that case—' Rick nodded '—let's grab our plates and join the party. I want to hear all about your previous career as a pastry chef.'

'Career? I could hardly call it that. My Elwood grandparents used to run an old *auberge* in Alsace. Yes. In the vineyard where they produce that dessert wine you enjoy so much. I might have picked up a few catering tips during my visits as a girl. And I do recall lots of family birthdays and weddings.'

Images of wonderful afternoons spent baking with her family flooded Saskia's memory and she chuckled out loud in delight for a second before her smile faded. Now she cooked and baked alone and she hadn't realised just how much she missed the companionship until that moment. How odd.

She blinked across at Rick and smiled. 'But that's very boring. Unlike your little speech to the guests just now, singing the praises of the bride and groom. I was impressed, Mr Burgess. And all in the most excellent French.'

'Why, thank you. I meant it. They have a great future ahead of them and the passion to go with it. All praise to that.'

Saskia stopped at the entrance to the stone courtyard, then turned away and strolled out to the edge of the garden and looked out over to the low hills covered in neat rows of grapevines, which she could just make out in the fading light. The ambers, golds and reds of the autumn trees and leaves contrasted against the green foliage of the conifers to create a lovely autumn scene. It was tranquil and serene and everything that she remembered about Alsace.

'It is so lovely. Are you planning to come back for the harvest?' she asked.

'Nope. I would only get in the way and I have appointments in Argentina with some amazing new wine estates. Nicole will let me know about yields and her first impressions when she's ready. I only hope they can relax on honeymoon for a week before coming back to the harvest. The weather forecast is looking mixed for the rest of the month but it should be a good vintage.'

'My goodness, Mr Burgess—' she smiled '—for a moment there, you sounded like a wine merchant.'

He burst out laughing and spun her around by twirling her waist. Then, before she could complain, he pressed his warm lips against hers and held them there for just a fraction of a second too long to be a friendly kiss between colleagues.

She might blame it on the atmosphere of the wedding and the beautiful setting, but it was probably one of the most romantic and lovely moments she'd ever had and it was so, so tempting to lean into that kiss and turn it into something else.

But that would mean giving into the sensation and letting him take over her life.

The Rick she had seen at this wedding and earlier at the chalet was so tempting. He was so charming, so handsome and so beguiling that her poor girlish heart yearned to see where that kiss might take them and not care about the consequences.

She had known all along that he was dangerous. From

the very start. But this was different. This time she wanted to be dangerous.

'You really must stop doing that!' Saskia protested and pushed him away. 'What if I kissed you in public?' she asked, pressing her hands on the front of his beautiful suit. 'How would you like it?'

'Like it,' he growled. 'I would write song lyrics and put posters up all over town with photographs to prove it.'

'You really are completely shameless. Do you know that?'

'It has been said. But it is a burden I have come to live with over the years.'

She rolled her eyes and shook her head. 'I give up. I relax and enjoy myself just this once and take a few hours away from work and I get pounced on. You see. This is what happens when I try to live in the moment or whatever it is you do.'

'Weddings. Happens all the time. Hey, you're a girl. What is it about weddings that makes every woman in the room turned back into a giggly schoolgirl and then go all weepy? And don't think I didn't notice you passing around the tissues during the service.'

'Do you really want to know or are you trying to come up with an excuse for kissing me?'

'I really want to know. And I don't need an excuse.'

'Okay then, I will tell you. Because, as you correctly point out, I'm a girl, and you are potentially going to become one of my wine merchants. Which, in my book, means that we should be open and honest at all times. And you can stop looking at me like that. I'm quite serious. Honest and open.'

'Right. If you say so. Should I be taking notes?' He patted his pockets as though looking for pen and paper.

'Right. That's it. I'm off to join the ladies and scoff desserts and chocolates. You are on your own.'

'I apologise. Please. I'm genuinely interested in your answer.'

Saskia looked into those grey-blue eyes, which were gazing at her at that moment with such an innocent expression that it was impossible to stay angry at him. Perhaps that was it? Perhaps he just beguiled ladies into submission?

'Very well,' she replied in a low voice. 'Weddings. A to Z. Key points.'

She gestured with her head towards the long kitchen table, where the wedding guests were laughing and singing and passing around desserts and wine. It was dusk now and the crystal glassware reflected back candlelight and the warm glow from lanterns hanging from the branches of the plane tree above their heads.

'I see this as a celebration. Look at this wonderful setting. Friends and family all gathered together having a wonderful time celebrating love and happiness.'

He shrugged. 'Great people. Food was good. Wine was amazing. Sounds like a pretty good combination for any party to me.'

'The food was better than good. It was splendid and I have several recipes tucked away in my trusty clutch bag. The wine was outstanding—as you predicted. Including the pink champagne from Chateau Morel, which was an inspired choice. And you're missing the point. This is not a dinner party or Christmas lunch or a birthday celebration or some other family meal. No. We're all here today to celebrate the love Jean Baptiste and Nicole have for one another.'

Almost as the words left her lips, the bride and groom slipped from their chairs and kissed lovingly under the lanterns to a great cheer before strolling down the table chatting to their guests.

'They are a lovely couple with such great hopes for the future. The future you...' she prodded him in the chest to get her point across '...are a big part of. You promised these two people an awful lot, Mr Bigshot. You had better deliver.'

'Don't you mean *we—*' he prodded her in the arm right back '—had better deliver? My best customer. Remember that?'

'How could I forget? I keep telling you that I'm still thinking about it, and yet you have reminded everybody several times of the fact that the heir to the Elwood name is on the case. I was starting to get nervous about my big build-up until I tasted the wine.' She sniffed. 'Not nervous now at all. It's a great choice. Brilliant. I wouldn't be ashamed to serve that wine to any of my guests; I'll give you that. But that still doesn't mean that I'll sign up with you. Not yet.'

Rick straightened his back and flicked off a small dry leaf from the jacket of his suit. 'Am I good? Or am I good?' he asked with a smile.

'If the other nine new generation winemakers are like this couple...then you're good.'

Rick responded by cupping one hand around his ear and leaning closer. 'Would you mind saying that again? I couldn't quite make it out.'

'I said that your scouting team have identified a suitable wine for the shelves of RB Wines. Congratulations.'

'Ah. Was that it? Thank you, kind lady.'

Then he snorted and pushed both hands deep into his trouser pockets. 'They're a great couple who have actually taken time to get to know each other. Which means that they are going into this marriage with their eyes wide open. Good luck to them.'

'Aha. I see,' she replied, her gaze still enjoying the happy scene on the patio. 'Things are beginning to become a little clearer. Do I detect a hint of personal experience there, Mr Burgess?' She laughed. Then looked back over her shoulder into Rick's face, and her smile was wiped away as a flash of regret and pain flicked across his eyes before he realised that she was watching him.

'My one and only engagement. Las Vegas. Four years ago. I'd been with Amy for six months and there wasn't an inch of that woman's body that I didn't know on a daily basis.'

Saskia groaned and lifted her hands to cover her ears. 'Oh, please stop. No details. I've just eaten.'

'Honest and open, right?' he replied and tugged her hands away. 'As I was saying. Six months. I thought I knew Amy. She was a sports journalist. Smart, funny, we both knew the same people and moved in the same crowd. Best of all, Amy was a total adrenalin junkie and loved going for the rush in extreme sports just as much as I did. Brilliant skier.'

'I'm waiting for the *but.*'

'We'd been to an Elvis wedding chapel ceremony with two Canyon climbers and in the spirit of the occasion and after several bottles of actually quite good champagne, I had a moment of weakness and decided that maybe getting married was not such a bad idea after all. It was a brave decision. The *but* came the day after our happy engagement when she cancelled a white water rafting trip because her parents had just sent her the latest property lists for her home town in the Midwest. Apparently they couldn't wait for us to relocate so they could be close to their future unborn grandchildren.'

Saskia stopped breathing and tried to speak, but ended up opening her mouth and closing it several times.

'Yeah—' he laughed '—that's right. I was engaged for a grand total of three days. Apparently my lovely Amy forgot to mention that in her opinion life as an adrenalin junkie was fine for single girls but the moment we walked down the aisle after the wedding, that was it. Forget the sports. Forget the old life. Forget all the reasons why we fell for one another in the first place.'

'I take it that this town was not close to any mountain regions.'

'Oh, Amy had that all sorted out. There was a climbing wall in the local school gym and cycling. Lots of cycling in this truly flat part of the Midwest. Great schools for the kids, though! And so close to Mom and Dad.'

Saskia exhaled slowly and whispered, 'Oh dear.'

'It got worse. I was crazy enough to agree to go and visit my future in-laws the day after we got engaged and, within half an hour of arriving at their mansion, it became pretty obvious that my lovely Amy had no clue about who I was and where my spirit lay. The crunch came when her dad offered me a nice secure nine-to-five job in his office supplies company over dinner that evening. I politely declined and made it clear that Amy and I would be moving very soon to California for my new career in the Burgess family wine trade.'

'How did that little bombshell go down?'

'Amy started crying and screaming about how selfish I was. The sisters started crying. Her mother started crying. And the father looked as though he was about to cry. I left when her aunt and uncle started to cry. Eighteen months later, Amy married a great bloke who was truly excited about a career in office supplies. In fact, I got a Christmas card from them last year, with a delightful photograph of the happy family and their two chubby toddlers.'

'She didn't know you,' Saskia whispered with her eyes downcast.

'And I didn't know her. She told me that she wanted to share my life as a professional sportsman but, when it came down to it, Amy wanted what her parents had. A quiet, steady life in a quiet town, with me working a steady day job. And I couldn't give that to her. We both dodged a bullet that would have killed us one way or another.'

Rick sighed long and low. 'Engaged for three days. That has to be a record.'

A peal of laughter rang out from the patio and Rick smiled and gestured towards the dining table. 'But these two? They've grown up together in the same small town since junior school. They know how the other person ticks and are building a life together and a future based on what they both want in their hearts. I believe in them and think they'll stick it out. Otherwise, I wouldn't have invested in a tiny vineyard like this.'

'This is their home. They love it.'

He blinked and shook his head. 'I couldn't do it. Stay in one place every day of every year and be content doing so. Not for me.'

'Why? What is so wrong with staying in one place and learning to love it? I love London and I love my home. I couldn't think of living anywhere else.'

Her voice tailed away. She thought wistfully of her old garden and all the work waiting for her when she got back. Even in this stunningly pretty vineyard, surrounded by people she would love to get to know better, she couldn't wait to get back and start in her settled life with her friends.

Rick turned round so that his whole body was facing her when he replied, those blue-grey eyes sparkling with excitement and passion with every word he spoke. In the light from the kitchen, the sun-bleached front of his hair contrasted with his tan to give him the air of a man who spent his days in the fresh air and sunshine.

'Have you never wanted to travel, Saskia? To see the world in all its glory? To watch the dawn come up over the Andes or climb up to Everest base camp and sleep on the glacier? You can hear the ice creaking underneath your tent as it slips away further down the mountain day by day. You can't replace that. The excitement. The buzz I get from paragliding or mountaineering. There's nothing like it. Nothing. I need that in my life, even if I have to break the rules here and there to make it happen.'

Saskia could see the pulse in his neck race as he talked about the life he led and just the way he spoke was enthralling.

He meant it. He would never settle down in one place. And in some ways she felt sorry for him. But envious at the same. She had never known that feeling of being free to do whatever she wanted and take off at a moment's notice.

She yearned to tell him about the exotic places her parents had dragged her to as a child, then leaving her in a hotel room with some stranger while they went out to a nightclub or beach party. That her mother had made sunbathing next to a pool into an art form while her academic daughter was left in the shade alone to read books. Neither of her parents ever had the slightest interest in the culture of the country they were visiting. Just the opposite. They went out of their way to keep things as English as possible.

She had learnt the hard way what being a tourist was like.

That was not her life—but it was his.

'You're not a great fan of staying in one place and making a stable home, are you, Rick?'

'Sure I am. I love my chalet. Let's just say that rules have their place but I have learned from personal experience that people who follow the rules often don't have a clue what they're missing out on in life until it is too late. I don't intend to let the rules get in the way of what I want to achieve.'

'And what about promises?'

'Ah. Now that, Gorgeous, is a very different matter. I make a promise. I keep it. No negotiation. No compromise. Done deal.'

'As simple as that? No second thoughts?' She smiled.

'No. Never. I have learnt to trust my instincts and go with my gut, no matter how risky it might look. If I make a mistake like I did with the lovely Amy, then I accept it with a good heart and move on.'

Saskia took a sharp breath before asking, 'Does that apply to the London wine store? Is that one of your risky ventures?'

'Not at all. I only take risks with my own skin and my own money. Not other people's. Promises, remember?'

Then Rick froze and his gaze scanned her face, his eyebrows crushed together, and Saskia felt that the air between them seemed to crackle with electricity before he tipped her chin up and looked at her straight in the eyes.

'Wait a minute. You said that this was a vanity project back in London. Is that what is holding you back? You think that I have spent two years making false promises to families like this one because of some arrogant whim to show that I can pull this off until the next tantalising opportunity turns up? Oh, Saskia. Just when I thought we were starting to work like a team. Sorry to burst your little bubble, but I have never been so determined to see something through in my life. I will create that store with you or without you. And I am in it for the long-term. Does that answer your question? Excellent. Because now it's over to you. The waiting time is over, Saskia. What is it going to be? Are you in or are you out? I am not having this discussion again.'

And before she could even think about an answer, he raised one hand and smiled across at the groom, who was gesturing for them to join them, and without a single glance he strode off.

She watched him back-slapping the young men gathered around the drinks table in the warm dusky glow as the women fluttered around like butterflies in their pretty summer dresses and heels.

He wanted her decision. No. He had demanded it.

Rick was a risk-taker. That was not going to change. It was what made him who he was and she had to respect that. Entrepreneurial. Adventurous and driven. Those traits were a fundamental part of his nature, which he had put to good use with his mentoring scheme and it was obvious to her that it would attract exciting new winemakers.

Rick knew what he wanted and was not going to change for anyone.

And she admired him for that, more than she could say. How many times had she gone the extra mile and had to change her plans to accommodate a so called pal or client and they had not shown the slightest gratitude? She had always been the one other people expected to change. Not the other way around. Anything to avoid upsetting people or letting them down.

If she agreed to buy wine from him then she would have to accommodate his attitude to taking risky decisions, which frankly bewildered her.

And maybe that would not be such a bad thing? She had been independent for so long. Perhaps it was time to shake things up?

Saskia was still thinking through Rick's question when Nicole strolled up to her in her long white lace wedding dress. She wound her arm around Saskia's shoulder and gave her such a loving hug that Saskia felt like crying all over again.

'Come and join the rest of us,' Nicole said with a smile. 'I'm so pleased that Rick brought you here today. It's so exciting to meet one of the buyers who will help us bring our wine to the world.'

'I've had a wonderful time and you have made me feel very welcome. Thank you, Nicole.'

'I'm glad. You know, twelve months ago we were unsure whether we would be able to invest in the new cellar equipment we needed. Then Rick came along out of the blue and suddenly everything seems possible. The mentoring programme, technology and the best advice we could ever want; it seems like a miracle.'

'It's a miracle to me how Jean Baptiste and Rick can jump off a cliff with a parachute strapped to their back. I was terrified this morning. Are you not scared?'

'Yes.' Nicole shrugged. 'But that's who he is. And I love him for having that strength and courage to live his dream. We are so different, but together we seem to balance each other out. We make a good team.'

Then Nicole tilted her head to one side with slightly raised eyebrows. 'I think you might know what that feels like.'

Saskia exhaled slowly and they both turned and looked towards Rick, who was on his hands and knees in his lovely suit playing hide and seek with the children under the table. 'I'm beginning to,' she replied in a low voice. 'But it might take me a while to get used to him.'

'Stick with it,' Nicole said and hugged Saskia one last time before stepping back. 'It has taken me six months to persuade Jean Baptiste to take one week away just before the harvest so we can have a honeymoon.'

'Congratulations. Where you going?'

Nicole blinked. 'We fly to Napa Valley tomorrow morning for a week-long international wine festival on the beach. All courtesy of Burgess Wine. Didn't Rick tell you?'

'No,' Saskia replied with a gentle smile. 'He never said a word.'

CHAPTER NINE

Must-Do list
- *Be sure to catch up with Kate about any new phone calls about bookings. Only had a few texts today—most unlike her. Probably out having too much fun.*
- *Email Amber about the new idea for the wedding arch—it could look gorgeous in January with the right flowers.*
- *Type up all of my notes on the outdoor wedding and place settings. Floral china is so pretty. But has to be top quality.*

'OF COURSE AMBER was delighted about my brilliant idea for the new wedding arch on my patio. Nicole and Jean Baptiste's wedding was so wonderful today—thanks to Rick for persuading me to go in the first place. Not that I would admit that, of course. I had to pretend that it was a networking meeting with two of his producers, but their wine is amazing.'

Saskia wiggled her shoulders back and forth and giggled like a five-year-old. 'It's been years since I have been so excited about changing my wine list and adapting my recipes to match. Oh, Kate, I really think that this could be the boost I needed to take Elwood House to the next level. It is going to be so magical that I can hardly wait to get started. Even if it does mean taking the risk and buying wine from Rick.'

'Magical. Oh yes. Absolutely,' Kate murmured.

'Do you remember that chocolate cake I made for your engagement party? The one you made me promise to make for your wedding? I might have found the perfect dessert wine to match it. We're off to visit the vineyard tomorrow in Alsace so I will be sure to bring a few bottles back for you to try.'

'Oh, great cake. Lovely.'

'You sound very absent-minded tonight.' Saskia laughed. 'Is work getting you stressed out again? Because, if it is, I can recommend some fabulous hotels in the Chamonix area.'

'Work. Oh no. No...' Kate replied as though she was finding the words hard to find.

Saskia paused. She knew Kate Lovat far too well—something was clearly bothering her but she wasn't talking. And that was not like Kate at all. Shutting her up was more the usual problem.

'Did I mention that Rick Burgess is prancing up and down on my bedroom carpet right at this very minute wearing nothing but a smile and that wonderful silk dressing gown you gave me as a surprise present? He looks quite charming in it. And that shade of cerise goes so well with his tattoos.'

'That's lovely... What? He's doing what? And where are these tattoos?'

'Um...I thought that would wake you up. Come on. What's going on? Tell me and get it over with. You know that I won't let you put the phone down until you do. Out with it, Lovat. What's bothering you?'

There was a loud sigh at the other end of the phone.

'Bully. I told Amber that you would want to know but we didn't want you to worry and spoil your trip.'

Saskia sat up straight against her bed head. *Worry? Spoil her trip?* Alarm bells started sounding loud and clear inside her head.

'Well, that is very reassuring. Come on, don't keep me in suspense. You know that I have a vivid imagination. Oh no. There isn't some bad news about Sheridan Press or your building permits for the new extension to your studio, is there?'

'No. Nothing to do with Amber or me.' Kate paused. 'You know we had a big storm last night in London? Lots of wind, gales, that sort of storm. And you know those really tall lime trees that are outside your bedroom window? Well, one of the branches might have crashed into your house and cracked an upstairs window and I am really sorry not to have told you earlier, but Heath organised a glazier and it's all fixed and as good as new. All done. That's it. That's the news. And I can breathe now.'

Saskia exhaled very slowly before speaking. 'The branch broke a window?'

'Cracked. Just cracked. No broken glass. All repaired. Nothing to worry about. Really. Heath organised the men who are working at our place to change the glass super-quick. And it wasn't raining…much. Sorry.'

Saskia closed her eyes and swallowed down hard. Then pressed her thumb and forefinger tight onto the bridge of her nose.

'There is nothing for you to feel sorry about. From the sound of it, you and Heath saved the day and were total heroes and I owe you one wonderful wedding in exchange. Thanks for being there, Kate. And thank Amber too. I am so grateful that you were there to help me out.'

'No problem. Have to scoot. My boy is back with the take-out dinner. Bye, angel. Have a wonderful trip and see you soon. Bye.'

Rick heard Saskia's footsteps stomp up and down the wooden floorboards in the other room and frowned.

He wasn't used to having overnight guests in his chalet, even pretty ones. This had always been the one place on earth that he called his private home.

One small spare bedroom. One kitchen diner and a cosy living room with a huge fireplace. Perfect for a young couple or a bachelor.

And, handily, not so perfect for his parents and their entourage, who preferred to stay at the local five-star hotel in Chamonix with its award-winning restaurant and spa facilities.

Of course Tom had just laughed and called it 'Rick's garden shed' and organised a high-tech Internet connection to be fitted at huge expense while he was away for a couple of days.

Chuckling to himself, Rick hunkered down and poked at the log fire which was burning brightly in the grate.

Saskia Elwood was a definite one-off. In more ways than one!

It had been quite a day and definitely time to relax with a glass of something special.

He settled down with his feet up on his comfortable fireside sofa, the music system playing a classical piano concerto, and was just reaching for his glass of Merlot when the door to Saskia's bedroom was flung open and she marched across the living room and stood in front of him, blocking his view of the fire.

Not that he was complaining because his new view was equally delightful.

Saskia was wearing a long silky dressing gown tied at the waist with a sash which begged to be tugged away. Her hair was down and messed up around her shoulders and her bare legs ended in toenails painted in the most interesting shade of coral, which probably matched her dress but he had not noticed before now.

But there was only one place which pulled his gaze and held it there in a fierce magnetic attraction he had rarely felt before.

His mother used to tell him that the eyes were the window of the soul.

Damn right. And right now Saskia's pale blue eyes were telling him that this soul was heading towards a very non-celestial place. Fire. Ice. Cool iceberg-blue. All wrapped in turmoil and anxiety.

In fact he was not astonished in the least when she lifted her chin and said in a quivering whisper of a voice, 'I can't do it, Rick. I just. Cannot. Do it.'

And then she burst into tears.

Sitting up straight on the sofa with Saskia's legs over his lap, Rick rubbed some warmth into her frozen bare toes by rubbing them gently between his palms. He had tried blowing on them but it turned out that the girl was a lot more ticklish than she pretended and she had almost wriggled off the sofa.

'How does that feel?' he asked, smiling across at Saskia, who was cocooned inside a warm fleecy blanket, sipping Rick's glass of wine. 'Any better?'

She replied with a small closed mouth smile. 'I want you to know that I am not usually such a mess.'

'Noted.' He nodded with a pretend serious look. 'Miss Saskia Elwood. London-based entrepreneur and expert dessert disher upper. Not a mess. Got it.'

He waited for her low chuckle to die down before raising his eyebrows and turning to face her. 'It was a broken window, Saskia.'

She groaned and covered her face with a sofa pillow. 'I know, I know. This is why I feel so totally pathetic at overreacting the way I did. And I really am sorry about blubbing all over you and your sweater. It was most unprofessional behaviour in front of my new wine merchant.'

Rick froze and then slowly turned his gaze to her feet, carried on rubbing her toes and gave a wide-mouthed grin. 'As my very first buyer, I am prepared to offer you this kind of customer service whenever needed. Good to have you on board. So you can stop groaning. If it makes you feel any better, I would like to think that we were friends before anything else. That works for me.'

She took a long sip of wine and flashed him a shy smile before whispering, 'Me too.'

'Excellent,' he replied with a twisted smile and covered her feet with the blanket. 'And now that is settled, you can tell me why one broken window is such a big deal and upsets you so badly. Between friends.'

Her head dropped back and the warm glow from the table lamps and the flickering firelight reflected back from the crystal tumbler in her hand before she slowly lowered it onto the coffee table.

Then, just as she was about to answer, Saskia gasped, grabbed onto his sleeve with one hand and pointed towards the window on the other side of the room with her other. 'Rick, look. It's snowing!'

Saskia threw off the blanket, wrapped it around her shoulders, slipped her feet into a pair of Rick's shoes and stepped out onto a long wooden terrace that ran outside the back of the chalet. And what she saw in front of her took her breath away.

The sunshine and dry crisp weather they had enjoyed at the vineyard had been replaced by heavy clouds in the cool night sky, creating a dark ceiling without moon or stars. And, stretched out along the long valley down below the chalet, was the picture postcard Alpine village that Rick called home.

The smell of wood smoke and pine resin filled her head with their musky, heady scents. Warm golden squares of light shone out from the chalet homes on either side of the river, interspersed with the occasional street light so that it looked like a long winding ribbon of Chinese lanterns which twisted away into the distance and the next valley.

And, falling straight down from the sky like a net curtain, were light flurries of large, fluffy flakes of snow.

It was like something from a movie or a wonderful painting. A moment so special that Saskia knew instinctively that she would never forget it.

And suddenly she understood why Rick had made this place his home. Of course. It was his refuge, just as Elwood House was hers.

She loved London, she always had. Elwood House was in a popular part of the city with a constant stream of traffic and pedestrians no matter what time of day or night. The contrast to where she was standing could not be greater. The village was quiet, tranquil and serene while her life seemed to be in constant turmoil.

She grasped hold of the polished wooden railing and looked out over the garden towards the mountains, her heart soaring, and she felt the anxiety of the phone call with Kate slip away in the exuberant joy of the view.

Up above them was snow and ice, while she felt safe and sheltered on this simple wooden terrace. It was icy-cold, snowing and her feet were turning blue but she did not want to move from the spot. It was truly magical.

It was almost a shock to feel a strong arm wrap her fleecy blanket around her shoulders and tuck it in and she turned sideways to face Rick with a grin and clutched onto the sleeve of his sweater.

'Have you seen this? It is astonishing. I thought the view from the top of the cable car station was spectacular, but this is wonderful. I love it.'

'I can see that on your face.'

Then he turned forward and came to stand next to her on the balcony, his left hand just touching the outstretched fingers of her right.

'You probably don't realise it, but there are very few people who I would invite to share this chalet. But you are one of them. You have a special gift, Saskia Elwood. I can tell from the way you describe your two friends that you care about those girls and then do something about it. I don't think that there is a selfish bone in your body. I admire that.'

'You admire me? What do you mean?' Saskia asked, taken aback by the tone in his voice. For the first time since they'd met, Rick sounded hesitant and unsure, in total contrast to the man who had been joking with his friends at the wedding.

Rick looked down at Saskia's fingers and his gaze seemed to lock onto how his fingers could mesh with hers so completely. 'These past two years have taught me that you don't know what life is going to throw at you, Saskia. You can't. I've learnt to take the opportunities that come along and enjoy them while I can, even if it does mean being totally single-minded. Selfish even. Always on the move. Filling the day with life and activity. That's the way I chose to live.'

Saskia looked into his face and remembered to breathe again.

'And how is that working for you?' She smiled.

Rick sighed low and long and shook his head briefly from side to side. 'My parents are still strangers trying to come to terms with losing Tom and I am not exactly helping by spending more time on the road than back at base. Chamonix is a long way from Napa.'

'That must be so hard, for all of you.'

He turned back and instantly switched on his smiley face.

But it was too late. She had taken a glimpse of who the real man was beneath the mask he wore in public. And the shock was, she liked them both.

'Oh, there are some benefits,' he replied, eyebrows high. 'It means that instead of freezing my important bits off climbing some mountain in Pakistan I am here in France enjoying time out with a lovely lady who might have a different take on life.'

He lifted one of Saskia's hands and kissed the back of the knuckles. 'I have even found the time to enjoy a vineyard wedding and a parapent jump on the same day. Imagine that.'

'Yes. Imagine. I was terrified this morning just watching you jump off that cliff top! I was almost too scared to watch you land. All your scars are testament to the adventures.'

Saskia turned back to the railing and gave a small shoulder shrug. 'I don't have that kind of courage, Rick, and I never will have. Yes, I am probably too generous with my time and my energy when it comes to my friends. But just the thought that there is a problem with my house makes me shake in my boots.'

She held both of her arms straight out at him. 'See.

Shaking. But it's all I have and I can't risk anything happening to it. That's why I totally panicked when I heard that it was damaged in the storm.'

'Why? Oh it's a lovely house and I was mega-impressed. But there are plenty of people who would have sold the place and used the cash to do what they wanted. Like go to university and study things that they are passionate about, or travel and find out firsthand what the world has to offer. Crazy things like that.'

Then he smiled. 'Don't give me that look. You have a good brain behind those pretty eyes and look hot in everything you wear. You could go anywhere you want. Do anything you want. So what made you decide to stay and rent out dining rooms in your house? What's keeping you in London?'

Saskia sniffed and dropped her head. 'Thank you but I think you already know the answer to that question, Rick. Let me give you a hint. Does the infamous Hugo Mortimer investment scam ring any bells?'

'Your dad made some really bad decisions and stole a lot of money from a lot of people. But they were adults and nobody forced them to put their money into bricks and cement. You were a child.'

'Nice idea in theory.' She cleared her throat. 'Shame it doesn't work like that. He was impulsive and arrogant and delusional and the rest of his family were simply supposed to go along with everything he wanted without question.'

She slapped her hand down hard on the wooden rail in anger and frustration. 'Do you know the worst part? I still have nightmares about the day he was arrested. The police came to our huge expensive house in three cars, lights flashing and sirens blaring like some TV cop show, and literally dragged my dad out of my mother's arms. I was about fourteen at the time and had no clue what was going on or why they threw him to the floor and were putting handcuffs on him…and I was screaming for them to stop. To leave my dad alone…'

Words became impossible because of the stinging in her throat and the blinding tears which blocked out her vision.

All she could feel was Rick's strong arms, which wrapped around her and held her tight against his chest with her head nestling into his shoulder.

He didn't say a word but she could feel his strength seep out from below his fine sweater and reach into her heart and quell her pain until she could suck in deep breaths between her sobs. She tried to slip her arms out but his grip only tightened in response.

'Hey, you can stay right where you are,' he whispered into her hair and snuggled in closer, his hands splayed out on her back. 'Take five minutes. Hell. Take as long as you like. No scars? You have plenty of scars, gorgeous.'

He slid one arm up her side and pressed two fingers flat onto her chest so they rested above her heart and she could feel the warm pressure of his fingertips through the wool throw. 'But they are not on the surface like mine are. They are all in here. And they hurt just as bad. Because I think other people pushed you beyond the limit of what you were ready to handle. But here is the thing. From what I've seen, the only perfect and constant objects in this world of ours are the sky, the oceans and the mountains. Everything else needs work and is likely to change at a moment's notice. And that goes for every single one of us.'

'Then how do we cope with all of that chaos?' Saskia blinked. 'My dad took everything my mother and I had, and more besides. We lost everything. Savings. Home. Everything that could be sold was sold. Don't you see? That's why I am struggling to make the leap into taking a risk on your new business. All I have left is my credibility and reputation. If I lose that by serving my guests anything but the best then I lose everything I have worked so hard to build up. I am alone, Rick, and I have to take the decisions alone. It is a huge gamble for me and I have learned the hard way that taking risks is a fool's game.'

'How do we cope?' he asked, his lips pressed against her temple. 'We do what our heart yearns to do or go to our graves full of regret and pain and loss for all of the things we didn't get to do and the words we did not say.'

'I'm not sure that I am capable of doing that.'

He responded by slipping back just far enough so that he could tip up her chin and tap her on the end of her nose.

'I've been watching you, Saskia Elwood. You are going to be astounded at what you are capable of. And if you don't succeed you learn from your mistakes and do what you have to do to get back up and try again until you can prove to yourself that you can do it. And then you keep on doing that over and over again.'

'No matter how many times you fall down and hurt yourself?'

'You've got it. Your Aunt Margot would be proud if she could see you now.'

Saskia turned her face and rested her cheek on his chest and looked out towards the horizon, suddenly needing to get some distance, some air between them. What he was describing was so hard, so difficult and so familiar. He could never know how many times she had forced herself to smile after someone let her down, or walked away without even thanking her after she had worked so very hard to please them.

Saskia blinked back tears and shrugged deeper into the fleece blanket while she fought to gain control of her voice. 'Some of us lesser mortals have been knocked down so many times that it is hard to bounce back up again, Rick. Very hard.'

Tears pricked her eyes and she swallowed down the pain to get the words out. 'I loved working in my aunt's wine shop after school and at weekends when my mother was away with her rich pals. But after my dad was arrested I couldn't...' She took a few short breaths before going on. 'I couldn't work there a minute longer. They knew it was nothing to do with me, and I was family, but...I just couldn't embarrass them like that. Do you understand?'

Rick replied by wrapping his long arms around her body in a warm embrace so tender that Saskia surrendered to a moment of joy and pressed her head against his chest, inhaling his delicious scent as her body shared his warmth.

His hands made lazy circles on her back in silence for a few minutes until he spoke, the words reverberating inside his chest into her head. 'Better than you can imagine. What did you do then?'

Saskia raised her head, laughed in a choked voice and then pressed both hands against his chest as she replied with a broken smile. 'I went to school every day and kept my head down and stayed in the background with my pals and made a life for myself with my Aunt Margot in Elwood House. What else could I do? My mother had run away to kind friends in Los Angeles to escape the press scrum and my aunt was the only one holding us all together. And I never left.'

'That was a long time ago, Saskia. What's holding you back now? Today? This minute?'

He tilted his head sideways to look at Saskia as she moistened her lips, her mouth a straight line.

'Isn't it obvious?' she whispered after several long seconds. 'Losing Aunt Margot hit me hard and I still haven't recovered from the shock. I'm scared.'

'Scared of what? Failure? Hell, girl, I've made so many mistakes these past two years I must have been the laughing stock of the wine business. Good thing I am able to laugh at myself and enjoy the journey.'

'How did you do that? How did you pick yourself up after losing your brother? Your parents must be so proud of what you have achieved.'

'Oh, girl. If only that were true. My mum and dad have never understood this compulsion I have to push my body and my mind through challenges which need high mountains and ridiculous adventures. I don't blame them for that. Far from it. Tom was always the academically gifted crown prince. The quiet, hard-working golden boy who could do no wrong. But me?'

A long shuddering sigh echoed out from deep in his chest and Saskia felt the wave of sad regret wash over her. 'I was a mystery to them as a teenager and I am still a mystery to them now. They know that I still resent being called back into the family business. Once a black sheep, always a black sheep. The problem is, I am the only black sheep they have left so they have to give me a chance and put up with me doing things my way.'

Saskia gasped. 'But you have worked so hard.'

'I am slowly persuading them that there is more than one way to get the job done.' Rick smiled, his face suddenly energised, the laughter lines hard in the warm light flooding out from the living room. 'And that includes trusting my gut reaction to choose who I work with.'

Then he shrugged and tilted his head slightly to one side. 'Here is an outrageous idea. I have already committed to moving my London office into Elwood House. Let me take that further. You need financial backing with someone you can trust. I need someone who can help promote the wine store. Why don't we combine the two? Let me invest in your business the same way that you are taking a risk and investing in mine.'

Rick pointed two fingers at her chest, folded his thumb into his palm and fired off a single shot. 'I choose you, Saskia Elwood. You are the woman I want to work with in London and nobody else will do.'

CHAPTER TEN

Must-Do list

- *Damn, but Rick is a good salesman and apparently does know a few things about his customers after all. The wine I tried today would be perfect for Amber's new wedding menu. Buy some before it is all snapped up by other customers.*
- *Last night in Chamonix and in the chalet. Perhaps take the rest of the night off. Need to be fresh and alert for journey back north tomorrow. Shame. I will miss this chalet.*

RICK STOOD IN silence, his gaze locked onto Saskia's shocked pale blue eyes as she took in a few breaths of the cool night air.

What had he just done? So much for playing it cool.

Rick inhaled very slowly and watched Saskia struggle with her thoughts, her dilemma played out in the tension on her face.

She was as proud as anyone he had ever met. Including himself. This was quite something.

And just like that, the connection he had sensed between them from the moment he had laid eyes on her standing outside Elwood House kicked up a couple of notches. And the longer he watched her, the stronger that connection became until he almost felt that it was a practical thing. A wire. Pulling them closer together.

And every warning bell in his body starting screaming *Danger* so loudly that in the end he could not ignore it any longer. And this time he was the one who snapped the wire binding them together and stepped back, away from her.

She shivered in the cool air, fracturing the moment, and he stepped back and opened the patio doors and guided her back into the luxurious warmth of the log fire and the living room.

'Say that again,' Saskia stuttered. 'I thought that you simply wanted me to buy your wine?'

'I do. This is extra.'

Saskia sucked in air, her shoulders heaving as her brain struggled to catch up. Then she flung her head back and glared at him though narrowed eyes.

'Extra? Wait a minute. When did you come up with this brainwave? Because the last thing I want is your pity just because I told my sad little tale. No, Rick. I am independent for a reason. I make my own decisions. Remember?'

His reply was to wrap both arms around her back and pull her to him in a warm hug before sliding his arms out and smiling into her face.

'I don't do pity. We have just been talking about taking risks and going for business opportunities when we see them. And I see one in you. It is as simple as that. I want to invest in you.'

'Me? Right. I think I need to sit down now.'

'We can do this,' Rick murmured as he stood behind her with his arms wrapped tight around her waist. 'And you know how much I like a challenge.'

'Is that what I am?' she asked and he could hear the smile in her voice. 'Another one of your challenges?'

'Absolutely. I might have to use every bit of technical

know-how I have to pull it off and get back to ground in one piece, but you're the girl I want to jump off the cliff with. Even if I have to strap you into that harness myself. No more watching from the sidelines. Not any more.'

'What?' She whirled around and looked him straight in the eyes and gasped, until she saw his smile. Then she thumped him hard on the chest. 'Oh, just for a second I thought you might be serious about the jump.'

'It might happen,' he said, blinking.

'No chance. I promised Amber and Kate when I left London that I would take care of myself and not do anything dangerous.'

She pushed her lips out and shrugged. 'Sometimes a girl has to keep her promises.'

Rick took one step forward and, before Saskia realised what was happening, he had wrapped his hand around the back of her neck, his fingers working into her hair as he pressed his mouth against hers, pushing open her full lips, moving back and forth, his breath fast and heavy on her face.

His mouth was tender, gentle but firm, as though he was holding back the floodgates of a passion which was on the verge of breaking through and overwhelming them both.

She felt that potential, she trembled at the thought of it, and at that moment she knew that she wanted it as much as he did.

Her eyes closed as she wrapped her arms around his back and leaned into the kiss, kissing him back, revelling in the sensual heat of Rick's body as it pressed against hers. Closer, closer, until his arms were taking the weight of her body, enclosing her in his loving, sweet embrace. The pure physicality of the man was almost overpowering. The scent of his muscular body pressed ever so gently against her combined with the heavenly scent that she knew now was unique to him alone.

It filled her senses with an intensity that she had never felt in the embrace of any other man in her life. He was totally overwhelming. Intoxicating. And totally, totally delicious.

And just when Saskia thought that there could be nothing more pleasurable in this world, his kiss deepened. It was as though he wanted to take everything that she was able to give him and without a second of doubt she surrendered to the hot spice of the taste of his mouth and tongue. Wine and coffee. And Rick.

This was the kind of kiss she had never known. The connection between them was part of it, but this went beyond friendship and common interests. This was a kiss to signal the start of something new. The kind of kiss where each of them were opening up their most intimate secrets and deepest feelings for the other person to see.

The heat, the intensity, the desire of this man was all there, exposed for her to see when she eventually opened her eyes and broke the connection. Shuddering. Trembling. Grateful that he was holding her up on her wobbly legs.

Then he pulled away, the faint stubble on his chin grazing across her mouth as he lifted his face to kiss her eyes, brow and temple.

It took a second for her to catch her breath before she felt able to open her eyes, only to find Rick was still looking at her, his forehead still pressed against hers. A smile warmed his face as he moved his hand down to stroke her cheek.

He knew. He knew the effect that his kiss was having on her body. Had to. Her face burned with the heat coming from the point of contact between them. His heart was racing, just as hers was.

Saskia slowly, slowly slid out of his embrace and almost

slithered off the sofa. And by the time she was on her un-
steady legs she was already missing the warmth of those
arms and the heat of the fire on her face.

'I think I've talked and been on my feet far too much
for one day. Now we really should get some sleep. Vineyard number three is expecting us tomorrow and with the
weather turning snowy it would probably be best to make
an early start and put snow chains on and...'

She knew that she was babbling but she had to do something to fight the intensity of the magnetic attraction that
she felt for Rick at that moment. Logic screamed at her
from the back of her mind. They were both single, unat-
tached, they were alone in the most romantic chalet that
she had ever seen in her life, and they wanted one another.

She had never had a one-night stand in her life. And if
she was going to do it, this was as good a place as any...
except, of course, it would never be casual sex. Not for
her. And, she suspected, not for Rick either.

Working together would be impossible if they spent
the night together.

Wouldn't it?

Rick stood up in one smooth movement from the hips
and instantly stepped forward so that his hands encircled
her waist. He gently drew her back towards him so that
their faces were only inches apart at the same height.

His hand moved to her cheek, pushing her hair back
over her left ear, his thumb on her jaw as his eyes scanned
her face, back and forth.

'The snow chains are already on. Don't lock me out.
Please.'

His voice was low, steady. And, before she could answer, his hand moved to cup her chin, lifting it so that
she looked into his eyes as he slowly, slowly moved his

warm thumb over her soft lips. Side to side. No pressure. Just heat.

She felt his breathing grow heavier, hotter and her eyes started to close as she luxuriated in his touch.

'Take a risk on me, Saskia. Can you do that? Trust me not to let you down?'

Risk? He was asking her to take a risk?

Her eyes opened wide and she drank him in; all of him. The way his hair curled dark and heavy around his ears and neck. The suntanned crease lines on the sides of his mouth and eyes. And those eyes—those amazing grey eyes which reflected back the flickering light from the log fire and burned bright as they smiled at her.

She could look at that face all day and not get tired of it. In fact, it was turning out to be her favourite occupation.

Rick the man was temptation personified. And all she had to do was reach out and taste just how delicious that temptation truly was.

Did he know what effect he was having on her? How much he was driving her wild?

Probably.

Shame that he had to go and ruin it all by asking the one question she had feared. The one question which would decide which path she would take in her life.

'Are we talking about the car journey to Alsace?' she whispered.

'Maybe. Maybe not.' He smiled as his gaze found something fascinating to focus on in her hair. 'What do you think?' He winked.

Saskia was about to retort with a polite refusal when she made the fatal mistake of looking into those eyes and was lost.

'Is that the way you usually interview business partners?' Saskia asked, trying to keep her voice casual and light. And failing.

He simply smiled a little wider in reply, one side of his mouth turning up more than the other, before he answered in a low whisper. 'I save it for cold weather emergencies. And for when I need to know the answer to an important question.'

'Hmm?' He was nuzzling the side of her head now, his lips moving over her brow and into her hair as she spoke. 'Important question?'

Rick pulled back and looked at her, eye to eye. 'I had to find out if you were seeing anybody at the moment. And now I know the answer, I can do something about it. So. Are you going to take the risk and jump into my car for a drive to Alsace tomorrow?'

Saskia leant back against the sofa and took another breath before grinning back at Rick. 'Well, I might. If you smarten yourself up a little.'

He bowed in her direction. 'Any time.' He dropped his hand and pushed it deep into the pocket of his denims. 'Would you care to join me for breakfast later this morning, Miss Elwood? No strings. Or do I have to use my emergency procedure again?'

'I might just risk your croissants.' She nodded. Then a warm sweet smile lit up her face. 'But, in the meantime, you can call your parents and tell them the good news. Elwood House has agreed to be your first paying customer. That should put a smile on their faces. Deal? Deal. Goodnight, Rick. Goodnight.'

Rick leant against the wood-panelled wall at the front of the dining room with a glass in his hand and enjoyed the view.

Saskia Elwood was on her third piece of Kugelhopf cake

and sweet dessert wine and savouring every mouthful, much to the delight of the elderly great-grandmother of the Alsace winemaking family who had made both of them.

They had spent a great day celebrating the grape harvest, which had been collected in perfect weather just before the frost, ending in a family party at the local *auberge*. And Saskia had been the star of the show every step of the way, from the very first moment she'd started chatting to the family in a perfect Alsace accent right through to her donning an apron to help out in the kitchen when there was an unfortunate incident involving their Labrador puppy, Coco, and some wild boar sausages.

They had eaten to bursting, danced until they couldn't stand and laughed. Really laughed. Saskia had made herself part of the extended family and dragged him along with her.

It had been a long time since Rick had felt so mellow and connected to a group of people who shared a common bond through the love of life and family.

Family. In the end, it all came down to that one common bond.

And one person was at the centre of it all. Saskia. His Saskia.

On the car journey from Chamonix to Alsace they had talked and laughed for hours. Sharing tales about their favourite music, food, friends, silly stories about their school days and people they had known. And yet they still kept coming back to the families who loved and exasperated them in equal measure.

Somehow Saskia had helped him to open up and talk about all of those memories from the happy times he had spent with Tom and his parents in Scotland and then California. Christmas parties and family weddings with all of the aunts and uncles, cousins and neighbours he had not thought about for years. Good times. Better times.

It was as though she had opened a window on another way of looking at the turmoil of the past two years and put it into some sort of perspective. This amazing woman he was looking at now had a father in prison and her mother was a stranger living her own life in another city, while he had two wonderful parents who were still grieving as much as he was.

Parents he was trying so hard to impress while all the time perhaps they simply needed him to talk to them.

Rick flicked open his cellphone, licked his lips and scrolled down to the number he had not called for days.

Now was as good a time as any.

'Dad? Rick. How is the weather in Napa today? That's great. Did Mum get those photos I emailed about Nicole and Jean Baptiste's wedding? Oh, of course. Too busy getting ready for the wine festival. Yeah. Just calling with two pieces of news. First—Chamonix has snow. I know, in September! But there's more. Do you remember me telling you that I was meeting with Margot Elwood's niece in London? Well, guess who is going to be my first serious customer for the new store? I know. I'm pleased too. Saskia Elwood is someone I can work with, I'm sure of it. Okay, I'm talking too much. Tell me about the festival. I want to hear all about it.'

Saskia stood in the front porch of the *auberge* where they were staying and waved goodnight to the last of the family of local winemakers who were still singing as they wound their way down the narrow lane to their homes in the village.

Most of the inhabitants of the Alsace village had gathered together to celebrate bringing in the wine harvest in the dining room of the *auberge,* and quite a few of the children too.

There were going to be a lot of hangovers and bleary eyes tomorrow morning. She checked her watch. Make that later *this* morning!

Thank goodness they all lived within walking distance. Or should that be staggering distance? It'd been a brilliant celebration and the winemakers had welcomed Rick with open arms. And when he'd announced from the front of the room that she was going to be their very first buyer of the new wine in London? She might as well have been an honorary member of the family.

Her feet had never left the ground since.

The food was spectacular, the wine amazing and the atmosphere? Oh, the people and the atmosphere had re-minded her more than any words could say of the tiny vineyard her Elwood grandparents had made their home. Working and living with people whose lives revolved around tending the grapevines they had inherited from generations of family winemakers before them.

Rick had been right. She did need to spend more time away from London and all the pressures that came with Elwood House. She used to love coming to Alsace as a girl to be with her family and yet somehow she never found the time to take a real holiday.

But what could she do? Her life was in London and her grandparents were long gone. How could she steal away for weekends and holidays and spend more time here?

A shiver ran across Saskia's shoulders. The crisp night air was cold enough for a light frost on the lawn and stars shone brightly in the inky-dark pollution-free sky.

Breathing in deeply, she was just about to turn away when she sensed Rick's presence behind her in the hallway, even before she had seen him. A feather-light duvet coat fell onto her shoulders and she wriggled deeper inside it.

Rick came up and stood beside her and she felt one arm wrap around her waist and snuggle her to him for warmth.

She sighed and tutted out loud. 'Aren't you cold?' she asked in a joking voice as she took in his shirt sleeves.

'Not a bit.' He smiled. 'This is nothing. And, besides, I've got a girl to keep me warm.'

'Have you indeed?' She play thumped him on the arm, which only hurt her hand and did nothing to him at all. 'Well, in that case, Mr Cool, thank you for the coat. It is too gorgeous an evening to say goodnight quite yet. Look at the stars!'

His reply was to pull her closer.

Saskia gazed up into his face. In the warm golden light from the porch she could make out the stubble on his tanned chin and upper lip and the way his hair curled around his ears and onto the pristine white shirt. It was so, so tempting to raise one hand and stroke that chin and find out if her memory of his kisses matched the reality of the man she was holding now.

Almost as if he could read her mind, Rick glanced at her and his dark eyelashes fluttered slightly in hesitation before he pressed his lips, those warm, full lips, against her forehead and held them there until her eyes closed with the sheer pleasure of his touch. It was almost a physical loss when he slid his chin onto the top of her head and exhaled slowly. She could feel his heart race to match hers.

Saskia closed her eyes and revelled in the sheer sensation of being held in Rick's arms. She wanted this moment to last as long as possible. To hold on to the glorious feeling that came with knowing that she was in the right place at the right time with the right person.

Especially if that person had a stubbly face and spectacular broad shoulders.

Rick Burgess made her heart sing just at the sight of him and her knees wobble at his touch.

How had that happened?

No. She was not going to overanalyse it. She was going to allow herself, for once, to relax and live in this moment. Not thinking about all of the things that she should be doing or planning for the next event.

Just living in the moment. And enjoying that moment to its full potential.

She had never truly done that before. Ever.

Ever since she could remember, her life had been one long series of lists of things that she should do or should not do, when to speak, what to say and how to act. To be released from that pressure felt magical.

And she knew just who to thank for showing her what her life could be like, given the chance.

The man who was holding her now. Rick the Reckless—who was not so very reckless after all. He was just…Rick.

This man had pressed buttons she did not know that she even had. And a few which surprised her. Shown her what being in love could be truly like.

She tilted her head so that she could look more closely at the pulse in his neck, his chest rising and falling.

She was willing to take that risk with this man.

Watching him now, his face relaxed, warm, handsome, it would be so easy to be seduced into the sweet and tender kisses of the man she had come to care so very much about.

Tonight had swept away any lingering, unspoken doubts she could have had.

This was what she had truly been frightened of, what she had always feared would happen when she gave her heart.

And she had truly given her heart, no doubt about it.

They had become attached with bonds you could not cut with a sharp tongue or kitchen knife.

She was doomed.

No. She would never forget him. His laughter. His teasing. His touch on her skin.

How could she walk away from this man? When she wanted him. Knowing that she was setting herself up for loneliness and pain if she walked down that road.

Rick stirred slightly and she grinned up at him. 'It was a wonderful evening. Thank you for making it possible for me to be here.'

Rick chuckled for a moment before answering. 'You are most welcome. I only hope that I can still dance like our host's grandfather when I get to his age.'

She slowly twisted her body around so that there were only inches between them, so close she could feel the warmth of his breath on her face as it condensed into a fine mist in the cold air.

The sound of laughter from the *auberge* owner and his family drifted out from the dining room and they both turned around to listen and then smiled at one another.

'I know. This trip has brought back so many happy memories,' she whispered, her voice low as she scanned his face. 'I'm only sorry that I didn't come back to France sooner. But, after Aunt Margot died, I felt that I had to keep busy. It is too easy to mope on holiday.'

Rick raised his hand and stroked her cheek with his fingertips from temple to neck, then back again, forcing her to look into his eyes.

'I know what you mean. Listening to you talk about your aunt has helped me realise that I have never stopped in one place long enough to get over Tom's death and grieve his loss the way you have tried to do. One more point to you, Saskia Elwood. Miracle-worker. '

Saskia looked up into Rick's lovely eyes as he gently stroked her face, before replying. 'Me? Not a bit. I prefer to think that France has worked its magic on both of us. I have always loved it here. And if it wasn't for my dad... well, perhaps my life would have taken a different turn.'

Then she pressed her fingers to his lips, her eyes never leaving his. 'But then, we might never have met. And my world would have been a much sadder place.'

Rick's response was to draw her body closer to his, so that her head was resting on his broad shoulder, cuddling into his warmth, sensing and hearing the pounding of his heart as she slid her arms around his waist.

She had no need of hearing.

No need of sight.

The smell of his body, dancing sweat, and him, his own perfume, combined with the smooth texture of his fine shirt above the powerful muscles that lay below to create a heavenly pillow.

So that when she finally dared to break the silence her words were muffled in his chest. 'I plan to make some changes in my life when I get back to London. Even with managing Elwood House. I want to take time for short breaks. Life is so short. These past few days have made me realise just how much I miss being back in France. There are second cousins still here and I haven't seen my mother since April. I don't know how I'll manage it, but I need to make it happen.'

'You'll do it. And don't worry about Elwood House. If you allow me to invest in the business, you could train a wonderful deputy manager. No problem.'

'Really?'

'Really really.' He smiled. 'Family has to come first. I only wish that I had realised it earlier.'

There was a subtle change in the tone of his voice and Saskia looked up as Rick's gaze fixed on the movement of wind in the pine trees and the stars above them. He had a faraway look in his eyes as though he was talking to the sky itself. His softly spoken words had the power to penetrate her heart and bring burning tears to the back of her throat.

'I never had a chance to say goodbye to my brother Tom.'

Rick's hand moved in gentle circles on her back.

'I was climbing in the Andes and out of reach of the rest of the world. No Internet, no cellphones, no bombardment and clamour of the world. No constant noise and clutter. It had taken us three weeks to walk in and acclimatise to the altitude. Which was just how I liked it. We were a small team who knew what we were doing and what we were up against, working together and pitting ourselves against the best. We were the best!'

Rick slowly lowered his gaze so that they were facing each other and Saskia felt the air between them chill even further.

'Everything is so simple on a mountain. She strips you down to your most basic essence. No prisoners. It is a battle of you and your skills against nature and everything that she can throw at you. In theory, that should prepare you for anything in the outside world. But let me tell you, when I saw that helicopter coming up over the horizon at our base camp on the glacier? Suddenly I had a lot more to worry about than falling into crevasses and frostbite.'

He cleared his throat and shook his head.

'The minute I jumped into that helicopter I had this aching raw pit in my gut and every instinct that I ever had was screaming out a warning sign in big red letters. I knew that I was in trouble. But I had no clue about what I was about to face.'

His cheek rested on her head and she could feel the intensity of the vibration in his words through her skin.

'It had taken my parents three days to track the expedition down and pay a helicopter pilot to risk flying in at those altitudes. Three days was too long. Not even a private jet and police escorts could get me back to Napa Valley any faster. Tom never came out of the coma and died several times in the hospital, but it would have been nice to say something to him before he took his last breath.'

Rick's words were coming in jagged bursts as though he was holding back suppressed pain and she longed to help him express how he felt, but she dared not in case the flood waters engulfed her once she released the dam.

'He knew that you cared about him. I could see it in that photograph you showed me in the chalet. You were close.'

'Tom was my big brother and I thought that he was invincible and would always be there for me to fall back on. And I was wrong. Wrong about a lot of things.'

He smiled and rubbed his cold nose against hers. 'But not any longer. You've made a change in my life, Saskia. Helped me to get a few things straight in my head.'

'Me? How have I helped you?'

'Jean Baptiste and Nicole are on their way to a trade fair in California which Tom created so that independent producers could showcase what they do. I should be there right now to help and support my parents. Burgess Wine is the main sponsor. I need to be there. But there is always some great excuse why there's a burning problem in Europe that I have to solve in person or the world will end.'

He held up one hand. 'Oh, don't misunderstand. I want this London store to happen and I need to be based in Europe to see it through. But the truth is more basic than that. The more that I think about it, the more I realise that I have been so determined to prove to the world that I'm not the black sheep of the family any longer that I have been burning myself out running around the world, while all the time my parents needed me to be with them. To help them come to terms with losing Tom as a family. And I couldn't do it. I wasn't ready to try and didn't have the tools I needed to make it happen.'

He exhaled slowly and very gently released his arms from around her body, and stepped slightly back. 'Which makes me a fool. My parents are in their sixties. They need me to be their son and to work with them to carry on Tom's legacy. Instead of which, I am acting like a stubborn child who refuses to put on the hand-me-down clothes my older brother used to wear and resenting every second of having to change my identity to fit into his shoes.'

Rick shook his head slowly from side to side and tapped her gently on the end of her nose. 'Well, that stops today, gorgeous. I am going back to Napa to build bridges and this time it's because I want to, not because I am the only option that they have left.'

Saskia stared out past Rick and fixed her gaze on the gentle waving of branches to and fro in the light breeze, which was a perfect match to the tornado spinning inside her head.

It felt as though she had been strapped onto a horse on a childhood nightmare of a merry-go-round, which had started whirling faster and faster until all she could do was hang on for dear life, knowing that if she even tried to get off she would be seriously hurt.

Only to be slammed to a crushing stop into a large solid object called real life.

He was leaving. Just like her father had left her.

She had always known that this was a temporary arrangement. One week. Seven days out of her life.

It was just so hard to say goodbye.

'Then you have to go back to your parents and show them that you are the better man.' She smiled into his face and blinked away her tears. Her body yearned to lean closer so that her head could rest against that broad shoulder, but she fought the delicious sensation.

She had to.

He was so close she could drown in the heady mix of his scent and the warmth of a body that wanted to be with her as much as she needed him to stay with her.

It was almost a physical pain when his hands started to slowly move down her coat until they rested on her hips. Slowly, slowly, she looked up into the most amazing grey eyes she had ever seen.

And in that moment she could see there was something more. Something she had never seen before. Something different. His unsmiling eyes scanned her face for a few minutes, as though searching for an answer to some question he had not the words to ask.

Uncertainty. Concern. Doubt? That was certainly new.

His right hand came up and gently lifted a loose coil of her hair back behind her ear, in a gesture so tender and loving that she closed her eyes in the pleasure of it.

He slid his fingers through her hair until he found the base of her neck. Drawing her closer, he lowered his forehead onto hers so that each hot breath fanned her face with its intensity.

'Come with me.' The sides of his mouth twisted for a second, but this time there was no quick laughter. 'We could be back in London in a week. Come on, gorgeous. Take a risk on me and come to California. You won't regret it. After all, you have nothing to lose.'

CHAPTER ELEVEN

Must-Do list

- *Who am I kidding? This trip to France has opened my eyes to just how much I love having someone to talk to—about everything, not just the girl things.*
- *Need to take some big decisions about how I want to move forward in my life—difficult decisions. Scary decisions. Has to be done and I know who I want to help me make them—Rick.*

SASKIA LIFTED HER head and looked into those amazing blue-grey eyes which were gazing at her so lovingly that she almost, almost gave in to the temptation.

Inhaling a breath of cool air, she lifted one hand and stroked his cheek, feeling the stubble of his soft beard under her fingertips and watched his chest lift as he responded to her touch.

He meant it. He wanted her to come with him. He wanted her to leave London and come with him and meet his family and…she felt totally overwhelmed and terrified.

Suddenly her world felt totally out of control. She was whirling and whirling. Her heart was thumping so hard she was surprised that Rick couldn't hear it.

'Nothing to lose?' she repeated, and her shoulders slumped. 'Oh, Rick. Why did you have to say that? Why?'

'Because it is the truth. What is it? What's the problem? Is it me? Or California? Talk to me. Tell me what is going on inside that lovely head of yours. Help me understand.'

'It's all too much. Too soon. I only met you a few days ago and now you want me to go to California with you? No. I need to slow down and…and I need to breathe. Breathing would be good.'

She closed her eyes and tried to fight back an overwhelming sense of panic.

Her head was spinning and a strange dizzy sensation swept over her. Cold, hot. Then cold again.

'Here. Come on. Sit down and exhale nice and slow. That's it. Deep breaths, exhale slowly.'

Rick half carried her over to an old wooden bench and she collapsed down on the hard rungs and felt the coat wrapped tighter across her shoulders by Rick's strong arms as he sat down beside her and hugged her tight.

'It's okay,' he murmured. 'It's fine. Everything is fine.'

'Fine?' she gasped in between gulping down air. 'How can it be fine? I haven't had a panic attack like this in years. Years! And it happens now. At the very time I am starting to see some success in my crazy life. I am such a mess.'

'Hey, girls tell me that I am too much for them all the time. I understand completely. '

She lifted her head and blinked at him, and Rick had the cheek to grin and wink at her. But when she took another breath, the dizziness cleared a little and then a little more until she could sit back against the hard bench and look up at the sky without feeling nauseous.

'You must think that I am a complete idiot,' she whispered, not daring to look at Rick, who was still sitting next to her so quietly with his arm around her waist. 'First you offer to invest in my business and then…then you ask me to fly off to California with you. I should be pinning a medal to your chest and adding you to my Christmas card list. And how do I respond? By almost throwing up on you. I am so sorry.'

'Don't be.' He smiled and hugged her closer. 'I get it. These past few days have been quite a rush. I'm used to it. You're not. That's all.' His voice warmed and he shuffled around so that he could tip up her chin and gaze into her face. 'You did warn me about your fear of heights and this is quite a jump.'

'How do you know that? What if I let you down and let myself down at the same time? I don't want to disappoint you, and especially in California in front of your family and the wine trade. All I have going for me is my family name and some experience in running Elwood House. The last thing you need is to be ridiculed for investing in an unknown.'

'Not going to happen. And how do I know that I have hooked up with a star? I can see it in your face. Your voice. The way you meshed with Nicole and Jean Baptiste at their wedding and right here, tonight, in the love you have for this community. I watched you. You can speak the dialect and they are not fools. They know that you are the real deal, just as I do.'

Rick smiled. 'You. Are not capable of letting anyone down. I have been around long enough in sports to trust my gut instinct and I have never been wrong. Nope. No trying to wriggle out of it now. We are in this crazy project together.'

Someone inside the *auberge* started playing the piano and the sound of the music drifted out of the porch and into the garden, but Saskia barely heard the music. She was way too busy trying to remember to breathe while she processed what Rick was saying.

Which was even more difficult when he stretched out

his long legs in front of him, apparently oblivious to the cold and the way the fine cloth of his suit trousers strained under the pressure of the muscled thighs below.

One side of his face was lit by the warm golden light streaming out from the windows behind their heads, bringing the hard planes of those high cheekbones into sharp focus. His powerful jaw and strong shoulders screamed out authority and presence. He was a man who knew what he wanted and was not prepared to take no for an answer.

'What do you say, Saskia?' he said, his clear grey eyes locked onto her face, his voice low and intense, anxious. 'Are you willing to give us a chance?'

'Are you only talking about RB Wines or Elwood House?' she asked, her voice almost a whisper.

His response was to slide his long, strong fingers between hers and lock them there. Tight. The smiling crinkly grey eyes locked onto her and a wide open mouth grin of delight and happiness cracked his face. 'See. I knew that you would work it out. No, I'm not. But hey, doesn't that sound good?' He lifted one hand and wrote the words in the air. 'Burgess and Elwood. Wine Merchants to the stars. It's a winner. And Saskia and Rick isn't a bad combination either. Kinda like that. California and then London won't know what hit it.'

Saskia inhaled a deep breath, trying to process the words, while his body was only inches away from her own, leaning towards her, begging her to hold him, kiss him and caress him.

She swallowed hard and tried to form a sensible answer. 'I thought you couldn't wait to leave the city and head back to Chamonix and your chalet?'

'Angie has an excellent project team in London who are desperate to show me what they can do without my constant interference. My parents need me more right now.'

Saskia let out a long slow breath as his fingertips smoothed her hair back down over her forehead and into the back of her skull. Making speech impossible.

Then his voice softened to warm chocolate sauce capable of melting the coldest heart. 'I wouldn't want to start that journey with anyone else but the girl I am with right now.'

London. The wine store. Elwood House. And a chance for love.

This amazing man was offering her the chance to create something wonderful and make all of those fantastical plans she had dreamed up with Aunt Margot a reality. This man who she had only met a few days ago, yet she felt that she had known him all of her life.

He was holding her dream out to her, and all she had to do was say yes and it would be hers.

'Think of me as your personal guide to having some fun. You need to get out of the house and I'd like to introduce you to winemakers all around the world. Say yes. Say that you will trust me and come with me.'

Trust him? Trust him with her life, her future. Her love?

'Get out of the house?' She smiled and blinked a couple of times to help clear her head. 'I don't know about that part so much. I shall still need to invest a lot of time in Elwood House if I want to see it fly. Even if you do have your London office there.'

'Elwood House? Oh gorgeous, think bigger for a moment. My family company have a wine empire to run, and believe me, they could use your skills. You could work for the family, be part of the family. It could be great!'

What? Hold up! 'What are you talking about? I have been working for years to develop the skills to run my own private venue. That's what I want. That's what I have always wanted.'

The sound of laughter broke through her thoughts and Saskia pointed to the red geraniums still flowering in the window boxes behind her.

'I spent years learning the trade in a place just like this with my grandparents before I went to live with Aunt Margot. I can cook, clean, work behind the bar, manage, do everything. But don't you see? It has to be my own place. My mother thought that she could rely on my dad to take care of her and her family. He was a charmer and a chancer and I don't blame her a bit for falling fast and marrying him. But it was a disaster, Rick. We were left with nothing when he left. Nothing.'

She sucked in a breath, hoping that he would fill the empty silence, but he just sat there, looking at her as she dug an even deeper trench to separate them.

'I need Elwood House. It's my rock. The one place that I can call my own. I cannot walk away from it. Not even for a few weeks. That's why I agreed to think about buying from a London shop. So that I could be close to home. I cannot risk letting it go. Not on...'

As soon as the words left her mouth, she regretted them. The man who had been holding her so lovingly, unwilling to let her move out of his touch, stepped back. Moved away. Not physically, but emotionally.

The precious moment was gone. Trampled to fragments.

His face contorted with discomfort, pain, and closed down before her eyes. The warmth was gone, and she cursed herself for being so clumsy. She had lost him.

'Not on someone like me. Right. I've got the message.'

His back straightened and he drew back, physically holding her away from him. Her hands slid down his arms, desperate to hold onto the intensity of their connection, and her words babbled out in confusion and fear.

'Let's not talk about it now. You have such a lot to celebrate over the next few days when your family are all to-gether for once in California. We can start work when you are back in London.'

He turned away from her now, and sat back against the bench, one hand still firmly clasped around hers.

'I am not your dad, Saskia. I have never taken a risk with anyone else's money or time. Promises. Remember?'

Rick ran his fingers back through his thick dark hair from his forehead to neck. 'No. I am not going to stop jumping off mountains or pushing myself to the limits in everything that I do. I thought that you understood that.'

The bitterness in his voice was such a contrast to the loving man she had just been holding, Saskia took a breath before answering. 'It's what makes you who you are. I do understand that. Very clearly. It just takes some getting used to.'

'Well, that is not going to change. No way.'

He paused and licked his lips and the world seemed to still. 'Tom died of a brain haemorrhage. What I didn't tell you was that he collapsed in an airport after a twelve-hour flight after six days of back to back meetings and presen-tations at a trade fair. I saw his diary. He would have been lucky to snatch a few hours sleep a night.'

He dropped his head back. 'Tom was a workaholic. Thirty-six years old and single. He collapsed running to collect his bag from the luggage carousel so that he could catch a connecting flight home in time for a morning meet-ing. Isn't that the most ridiculous thing that you have ever heard? I miss him every day and think about him every day and I'm not ashamed of saying that out loud.'

Before Saskia could swallow down her tears in a burn-ing throat and form her reply, Rick slid his fingers from hers and got to his feet. He spun around to face her, block-ing everything else out of her sight.

'Is that how you want me to live, Saskia? Is that the kind of man you want to be with? To work with? Because, if it is, then you are absolutely right. I am not the man for you. But I do know one thing.'

He stepped forward and took both of her hands and drew her to her feet in one smooth movement so that they were standing chest to chest, thigh to thigh, with only the cold night air separating them.

'I know that you are an amazing woman with so much compassion and intelligence and passion in your heart that I cannot get enough of you. We are two of a kind, Saskia Elwood, and I want you in my life—but you have to make that decision. You know who I am. You know where to find me.'

And, with that, he released her hands, tilted his head and kissed her lips with a touch that was so light and so warm and so heartfelt that she staggered under the weight of it. So that when he stepped back she had to lean against the bench for support.

'Goodnight. And thanks for a great day.'

'No problem. Goodnight, Rick…' she whispered as he turned and strode away. *Or was that goodbye?*

CHAPTER TWELVE

Must-Do list
- *I miss Rick so much and he has only been gone a few hours.*
- *Maybe I should make a list of all the ways that I don't need him and how very different we are?*
- *Stupid lists. Forget the lists. I don't need to write down what I want and who I want. Not any more.*

RICK SLOWED HIS car to a stop on the brow of a hill and looked out through the windscreen as dawn broke over the valley stretched out in glorious autumn colours.

He had been driving for almost an hour and was already bored of his own company. Every music track on the radio or CD reminded him of Saskia and the echoing silence in the car as he sat there only made it worse.

The laughter and excitement of the previous evening seemed such a long time ago but he wanted to keep hold of that feeling of happiness when he'd held Saskia in his arms and capture it for ever to keep him warm in the cold winter months ahead.

Rick dropped his head back against the leather seat and closed his eyes.

He should be grateful and happy that his plans were coming together.

Instead of which, his mind was in turmoil and he had spent most of the night tossing and turning, trying to work through what it was he truly wanted.

The more he thought about it, the more he admired Saskia for having the strength to know what she wanted and make the sacrifice to create something remarkable from what she had been given. He was lucky to have met her. Know her. Care about her. *Start falling for her.*

Oh yes. He was falling for Saskia Elwood—and falling hard and fast. *Avalanche speed.*

And now he was driving away from the woman he wanted because he was scared of not being worthy of her. Or not being the man she needed in her life.

He was actually *worried* that he would let her down.

Which made him the biggest fool in the world.

Sunshine flickered at the corner of his vision and he half opened his eyes with a smile and a snort. He had faced some amazing challenges in the sports world and only a week ago he would have shouted out that he was ready for anything life could throw at him.

Well, a pretty brunette had just shown him how wrong he could be. About a lot of things.

One thing he did know. Whenever he needed to prepare for a big sporting event, he called in a support team who would back him up at every stage. Maybe it was time to call in Team Burgess? The one team he had left behind to go solo for the past two years.

Rick flicked open his phone and dialled the number.

'Mum? Great to hear your voice. Me? Been better. Fact is, Mum, I need your help. And this time it's not about grape varieties.'

Saskia stepped out of the side entrance at the *auberge* and her gaze scanned out across the lawn, which was edged with bright flower beds to the low hills that lay beyond.

Her breath condensed in the cold damp air into a moist pale mist in front of her face, as she opened the gate and strolled out onto the narrow path that wound its way through the vineyard. The glistening frost which covered the hard and apparently dead wood of the harvested grapevines was just visible in the early morning light.

She ran her fingers across one precious vine to the next, bracing herself with each step on the loose pebbles and stony ground of the slope beneath her feet. The earthy aroma of leaf mould, soil and sweet juice from crushed fruit wafted up as she slowly moved along the row, filling her senses in the damp air.

Some people loathed autumn, but she loved it. The chill damp of mornings like this one would open out into bright sunshine for a few precious hours later that day.

A shuffling noise and a cold wet nose pushing at her right hand broke the mood. 'Okay, Coco. Yes, I know it's breakfast time.'

Saskia strode back towards the house as the chocolate Labrador sniffed along the path ahead of her, looking for the rabbits, real and imaginary, with whom she shared the hillside. Sometimes she missed having a dog around, but it would be impossible in central London and with the kind of work she had chosen and the life she led.

She loved Alsace, she loved the culture and she loved the old family *auberge* where she had spent a sleepless night tossing and turning, her mind reliving every second of the time she had spent with Rick over the past few days.

Saskia shook her head and sighed. Stupid girl. She was getting too old to have crushes on hunky sportsmen...because that was all it could be. A crush.

But, lying in bed last night, trying to get some sleep and failing, Rick's words kept rolling around inside her head and simply would not go away.

Could she sell Elwood House and move to France? Or work for a company like Burgess Wine and employ a manager to run the venue? It would mean accepting Rick's offer to invest but it could open up all kinds of options that she had not even considered before.

Time was so short. The Christmas bookings were already coming in and then there was Amber's wedding and then Valentine's Day, mixed in with business meetings every week. Soon her life would be back to one long blur of activity and a holiday would seem like a distant dream.

No. She would make it happen. She could make the time for regular breaks. She had come a long way from the schoolgirl who was so terrified of drawing attention to herself in case the teasing about her father started up again.

It was time to start living a little.

Kate and Amber would be delighted and probably very creative when it came to setting up her social calendar!

Saskia picked up a small stick and threw it out to the stone wall of the terrace, watching Coco bound ahead to fetch it as she walked slowly back to the dew-frosted cobbled patio which circled the *auberge.*

Smoke from wood-burning stoves rose white and thick from the chimneys of the traditional timbered houses built along the path of the river valley below her. There was no breeze this morning to break the heavy cloud cover and chilling mist. That would come later with the seriously cold weather forecast for the rest of the week.

Coco ran back and forth into the vines and it was a few seconds before Saskia raised her head as her knees bent slightly to take the steeper sections of the slippery mesh of stones, worn smooth by generations of wine growers and their carts.

A warm smile blossomed on her lips as she grew closer to the house but the silence of her stroll was interrupted by the musical chime from her cellphone and for a moment she thought about answering it, before turning it off and indulging in a precious few moments of tranquillity before heading back to the long list of tasks that she had set herself to do today.

Just this once she would break her habit and ignore the siren call of her phone. And she knew just who was responsible for that.

Rick had already gone back to California to be with his family and she wished him well. He certainly had a lot of bridges to build. But she missed him so much already she had to keep busy or be a misery all day. His car was not in the car park so she had better make a start on working on transport back to London.

Saskia called out to Coco and they jogged down the path together. She had barely time to slip off her jacket and pet Coco when a very familiar voice echoed out from the warm country kitchen.

It couldn't be.

Stunned, Saskia wandered into the kitchen and stood frozen at the door.

Rick was wearing his smart casual denims and good shirt and his favourite boots, looking not only rested and handsome, but annoyingly chirpy.

How dared he stand there chatting to the breakfast cook? He must have driven to Chamonix and back again but he looked fresh and ready to take on the world. While she had tossed and turned half the night.

'Good morning, sweetheart,' Rick said. He picked up her hand and kissed it before winking at her. 'Look at you. Gorgeous as ever. You don't mind if I call you sweetheart, darling, do you? Excellent. That's my girl. Now—where can I find my breakfast?'

He pretended to look around, which was a joke since

the breakfast buffet table had already been laid out a few feet away in the dining room.

His girl? Gorgeous?

Saskia glanced down at her outfit and then narrowed her eyes at Rick.

She was wearing casual trousers which had picked up a thick layer of mud on the hems, her jacket was covered in dog hair from Coco and her hair was damp and limp around her shoulders. He couldn't have waited ten minutes until she had her shower?

'Oh, forget the breakfast. We can eat on the way.'

And then he launched himself at her.

Grabbing her around the waist, Rick pulled her to him as though she was water in the desert and kissed her so hard on the mouth that all sensible thought was wiped out.

There was nothing she could do except open her arms wide.

She didn't have any other choice. She was carrying Kate's gloves in one hand and a dog lead in the other. She couldn't even fight him off.

But then the kiss softened, one of his hands moved further up her back and his head tilted slightly so that he could lean in even closer.

This was it. This was the real thing.

This was Rick and it was everything that she had been hoping for.

As her eyes closed and she fell deeper and deeper into a hot kiss with each snatched breath, she was vaguely aware that the gloves and lead must have hit the floor because her hand slid up inside Rick's leather jacket and she returned the kiss.

His hands splayed out on her back as she poured into her kiss all of the passion and devotion, the fear and the doubts that came with giving your heart away to another human being.

It was total mind-numbing bliss. And felt so right it was crazy.

This was what she had been missing.

This was what she had been longing for since the moment he had said goodnight.

He was back and that was all that mattered.

Wait a minute!

He was back.

'Did they cancel your flight?' she whispered into the corner of his mouth.

Rick replied by bending his legs, grabbing her behind both knees and hoisting her over his right shoulder as though she weighed nothing at all.

'No time for that. I'll explain on the drive.'

'Put me down! Drive? What drive?' Saskia cried, clutching onto his jacket for dear life as her head bobbed up and down.

'The drive back to London, of course. It's time for you to meet my folks. They vet all of my girlfriends these days but they're fairly busy with a wine show this week so I am taking you to Napa to get some sun.'

'Wait! I haven't even packed my bag—and what do you mean—girlfriend? I thought you said that I was too set in my ways. Too much of a stay in one place kind of girl for an adventure junkie like you. Well, I have news for you—that hasn't changed. I'm still a home girl and I have no intention of changing that fact.'

'Great! Just what I need,' he replied and strode out down the hallway, much to the amusement of the family, who suddenly appeared out of nowhere as though they had been hiding. Even Coco wagged her tail—traitor!

'What? How can it be great? And can you please put

me down so that I can see your face when I am fighting with you?'

'Nope. From now on it's me and you against the world, gorgeous. I am not letting you out of my sight.'

Saskia looked up just as the *auberge* owner appeared at the door. 'Help! I'm being kidnapped.'

He replied by shaking his head slowly from side to side with a huge grin on his face before turning back inside.

'This is not funny,' Saskia called out in vain.

'Yes it is,' Rick replied and grinned around at her. 'Time to get you home, my sweet. We have a lot to do.'

'Wait a minute! I need my suitcase! And what do you mean, a lot to do?' Saskia replied as Rick bounced along the car park.

His feet slowed and she could see the back bumper of his four-by-four.

'I've had a busy morning. Apparently my parents are amazingly proud of what I have achieved so far. What's more, and you are going to like this, they are totally delighted that I am flying my new girlfriend out to meet them. That's you, by the way.'

'Girlfriend? Oh, Rick,' Saskia replied with way too much of a quiver in her voice. 'You told them that I am your girlfriend?'

'Absolutely. Because, incredible as it seems, I have come across a new extreme sport. It's all packaged in the shape of a girl called Saskia Elwood Mortimer. Dangerous? Hell, yes. But I am willing to take the risk.'

Rick stopped moving and took firm hold of her legs but when he spoke his voice was low and warm. 'So. This is the way it is going to be, Saskia. I am going to put you down, you are going to go inside and get packed. Then we are going to enjoy some excellent breakfast and drive to London together, before catching that flight. That's right.

I'm not letting you go. From now on I will be staying in one place. And that is where you are. No more running around the world. I am done with that. The Burgess and Elwood Show has come to town. Or...'

All she could hear was the birdsong in the pine trees either side of the road and the sound of Rick's breathing and the fast beat of his heart.

He was nervous. And she was heavy. Or both.

'Or...' she repeated with a quiver in her voice.

'Or you tell me that you don't want to be with me and I drive away and leave you here and I don't see you again.'

'Rick! No!'

His hands slid up her legs and gently, gently, gripped her around the waist and physically lifted her forward so that he was holding her under her bottom, taking her weight. And all the time his eyes were locked onto hers.

Then, and only then, did his grip relax so that she could slide down against the front of his shirt and jacket.

She didn't care that the front of her top had ridden up and was showing her pasty white midriff and back to the world on a cold frosty morning.

She cared even less that her trouser buttons seemed to have become snagged on his belt.

All she cared about was this man who was holding her and gazing at her face with such tenderness and love and devotion that it melted her heart just to look at him.

'Repeat after me,' he whispered in a voice that was hot chocolate sauce over home-made vanilla ice cream. 'I want to be with you, Richard Burgess, and the idea of being your girlfriend is growing on me. In fact I like it just fine.'

'I do like it,' she tried to say but her voice cracked and tears started streaming down her cheeks. 'Yes, I want to be with you so very much. Take me back to London, Rick. But only for as long as it takes me to get packed. I want to see California. I want to meet your parents—and most of all I want to see them with you.'

And then speaking was impossible because he had swooped her up, her arms still around his neck, and was twirling and twirling and twirling and laughing as though he wanted the whole world to know that she loved him.

'I don't want you to stop but I am getting dizzy,' she called out, deliriously happy.

'Best get used to that feeling.' He grinned and kissed her and it was the kiss of a man who knew what he was doing. 'From now on your feet are not going to touch the ground.'

EPILOGUE

Saskia stood in the conservatory room at Elwood House and looked out onto the snow-covered patio winter wonderland where Amber and Sam would have their wedding photographs taken.

The snow had been falling for three days. It was fluffy, soft, crisp and beautiful and the air was cold enough to glaze the covering with a sparkling frost that would twinkle in the white fairy lights Saskia and Rick had finished just in time to drive back to Alsace to celebrate Christmas with his parents and her mother.

Inspired by the bower of fresh flowers and grape leaves that she had seen at the wedding in France, she had worked with the florist to create an extension to her garden pergola of wire and woven fir tree branches cut from the garden of the *auberge*.

Tall enough not to bash Sam on the head, the wide curve was smothered now in gold cones and red berries and fruit and dark shiny holly leaves interspersed with trailing golden blossoms which would only last the day in this chill but were worth it.

At dusk the lights hidden in the miniature conifers on each side of the cleared paving would create a secret pathway to the lover's bower.

She had always thought that Amber was ethereal, but

this was her chance to make Amber's day truly magical. It was exactly how she had imagined it would be. And Amber had cried for ten minutes when she'd seen it yesterday which, of course, set the other two off.

Thanks heaven that Sam, Heath and Rick had taken one look at their weeping ladies, who were hugging onto one another over chocolate ice cream and champagne, and decided to take off to their boutique hotel across the square in search of a solid Italian meal which involved lots of carbs washed down by copious quantities of good wine.

But that was okay. The girls were allowed to cry on the day before the wedding.

It had been a manic few days of post-Christmas hairdressers' appointments, manicures and facials—for all three of them. Final fittings at Katherine Lovat Designs, emergency phone calls around the world to check on flight times to arrange airport pickups, courtesy of Sam's dad and his wonderful limo service, daily crisis meetings in Saskia's kitchen over chocolate cake to cope with stressful family members from all sides, but at last it was done.

The first one of their little band was marrying the man she loved. Amber's wedding day had arrived.

Saskia strolled slowly back to the main entrance hall, smiling at the caterers and waiting staff who were putting the final touches to the wedding reception dinner. The dining tables had been dressed with lengths of bright scarlet and gold wedding sari fabric with gold decorations, candelabra and detailing. The marble hallway and wide wing staircase was gleaming and splendid. An army of florists had transformed this old house into something which was better than any grand hotel Saskia had ever been to. And, even better, it had taken Amber's breath away when she'd first seen it.

Pillar candles with rich gold and scarlet floral decoration spilling out from crystal vases. Rings of intertwined ribbon flowers and eucalyptus adorned every chair and Amber's favourite flower, the orchid, stood tall in stunning planters on the console table and bookcases.

The overall effect was warm and welcoming—just what Amber and Sam had asked for. No stuffiness. No hundreds of wedding guests they did not know. No formality of any kind. This was their very personal and private celebration of their love. And not even Amber's mother Julia had been able to make her move an inch.

Amber's bouquet was made of a trail of gold orchids and pastel blossoms and leaves. The girl who had once been too shy to wear anything but dark colours and school uniform had been transformed under the sunlight of Sam's love into a daring and beautiful woman who celebrated the new home she had made in India.

The house almost did her justice.

After the reception, when the candles were lit and the lights dimmed, it would be remarkable. It was already remarkable.

She had never seen the house looking so amazing—so happy and splendid.

Saskia blinked nervously and scanned the checklist. This was it. After so many months of work and planning. The first wedding Elwood House had ever seen, but not the last if her plans came to fruition. Kate was getting married at Jardine Manor but there was only place she wanted for her English wedding to Rick—right here. In her own home. With her family around her, old and new. They could celebrate later at the chalet in private.

'Hello, gorgeous,' a familiar voice whispered and she turned to see Rick strolling into the kitchen holding a substantial-looking sandwich. 'Nice place you got here.'

She closed her eyes and exhaled slowly before holding

out the sides of her sweater and making a short curtsey. 'I'm pleased that you like it.' She smiled, but then her smile faltered. 'I'm only sorry that Aunt Margot never got to see it like this. She would have loved it.'

'Hey,' he said, and wrapped his arm around one shoulder and planted a tender kiss on the top of her hair. 'She would have been proud of you. I am. Except for one tiny little thing.'

'Only one?'

He turned to face her and tipped her chin up with one finger. 'You have never stopped since we got back from France. Time to take five minutes and join in the fun.' He gestured with his head towards the stairs. 'Go on up and do some of that girly stuff with your pals.'

'But what about Sam…?'

Rick held up one hand. 'Heath Sheridan is as bad as you are with lists and timetables. He'll walk Sam over from the hotel in good time for the wedding. Fear not, for the sake of the lovely Amber, our boy Sam is even prepared to talk to his scary future mother-in-law so I don't think he'll make a run for it. He's been waiting a long time to claim his bride. And I'm not going anywhere. Not when you're around and there is enough food and most excellent wine to feed an army back there.'

'Good to know that your priorities haven't changed.' She laughed, and then checked her watch.

'Oh no,' she gasped. 'I can't believe it's that time already. The first guests will be here in half an hour and I need to change and… Speaking of which,' she added, glancing down at his well-worn denims and T-shirt, 'I like your outfit. It's so you!'

He turned her shoulders towards the stairs and patted her bottom. 'Go. Chill. I'll come and find you in ten minutes.'

* * *

Saskia walked into her bedroom, which had become the makeshift Bride's Suite, and stopped at the door and inhaled sharply.

Kate and Amber were lying on her wide bed in their dressing gowns. Giggling and making duvet angels.

They were her best friends in the world, and one of them was getting married today. In a few hours their lives and their relationship were about to change for good.

This was the last precious time to be together as three single girls.

And right now they both looked just the same as the first time she'd met them at high school. Twelve years old and mad as a bag of frogs.

She blinked happy tears from the corner of her eyes, but she flopped down at the bottom of the bed, untied her tennis shoes, then stretched out on the bed next to them with her arm around Amber's shoulder.

'Hello goddesses,' she said. 'What's new?'

'There is some crazy rumour going around that Amber is getting married. Just thinking how ridiculous this all is.' Kate giggled. 'Want to join us before the hysteria sets in?'

'Absolutely,' Saskia said, and took a good long sip out of the glass of champagne on the bedside cabinet which, judging from the lipstick stains, belonged to Amber.

'Why did I ever think that New Year's Day would be a good time to get married?' Amber asked with a glazed look in her beautiful eyes and perfect make up. 'Everyone is still stressed out from Christmas, my third stepdad is stuck in a snowbound airport and my mum never stops reminding me about all the important celebrity New Year parties that she sacrificed to be here with me. And I am so terrified that I will fluff my lines it's ridiculous. If it wasn't for Sam, I'd be on the next plane back to India.'

'What, and miss all the cake,' Kate laughed and turned on her side to look at them. 'Relax, gorgeous. Your diva mother is having the time of her life and wait until you see the over-the-top outfit she is wearing! The hat is so large we can all shelter underneath if it snows again.'

Amber squeezed her hand and chuckled. 'I know. It's horrendous. And I'm sorry for being such a nuisance. You would think that I should be used to performance anxiety by now. It's just that…I'm getting married today.'

Then she blinked. 'It's finally happening. I'm getting married. Today. Isn't that amazing? And I think I am going to cry again now.'

'Not post-mascara you don't,' Saskia replied, then sat up on the bed and turned towards Amber. 'Deep breathing. That's it. Pretend that you are about to play the piano in front of your family and friends and they all love you. Kate! I leave you alone for a few hours. How many glasses of champagne have you two had?'

Kate slid off the bed in her stockings and rattled the bottle and peered at the couple of inches left in the bottom. 'Oops. Perhaps this is a good time to get the camera out before we finish it off and everything goes a bit lopsided. Sam's journo pal might be doing the actual wedding photos but I would like one of the three of us getting ready.'

'Give that to me, you scamp,' Saskia called out and rushed around the bed to try and snatch the small digital camera. 'You are not to be trusted.'

'Oh no, you don't, Elwood. For the past few months you have been running yourself ragged and getting used to being adored by a handsome stud, which is exhausting enough for any girl. Well, as of right now, you have to turn off your compulsion to control the world and enjoy yourself. Tell her, Amber.'

'Kate's right. Put the organiser and the camera down

now, Saskia. And I am the bride so you have to do what I say.'

Saskia stopped playing with Kate and planted a hand on each hip, then shrugged at Amber, who was sitting up against the headboard with her hands in her lap.

'You are. And I do. Look—organiser in the drawer. There it goes. All gone.'

'Now you have to close the drawer,' Kate said, looking over her shoulder. 'Go on. It'll be fine on its own. Besides, it would never fit in that tiny bag I picked out for you.'

'This is true.' Saskia grinned and sat down on the corner of the bed with Kate sprawled next to her and she reached out and took Amber's hand.

'Are you ready to get married now, lovely girl?'

'No. But I am ready to get married to my Sam. I love him so much it's crazy.'

'Then it's a good thing that he has officially redeemed himself by worshipping you for the goddess that you are,' Kate sighed. 'In fact, Sam is almost worthy of you.'

'Wow. Now that is quite a compliment. Ladies, I think this calls for a toast. Oh—no spills on the duvet. Excellent. Wait. I'll prop the camera up on the desk and set the automatic timer. Smile please—cheesy grins all around.'

'Oh, I'm blinded!' Kate yelled a microsecond after the flash went off.

Amber lowered her forehead onto Saskia's shoulder and, as she smiled with a quivering upper lip, a single tear slid from the corner of her eye onto her beautiful cheek.

'This has been some year—and I couldn't have got through it without you two,' she whispered.

'We're so happy for you, Amber.' Kate sniffed and dabbed the tear away before blowing into the tissue. 'You have waited eleven years to find out that Sam is still madly in love with you. That's mega.'

'Mega.' Amber nodded and reached for another tissue. 'You have your Heath and now Saskia has found Rick. Who would have imagined so much could change since the high school reunion?'

'Now don't get me started,' Saskia said. 'The three goddesses will always be the goddesses, no matter where we are or what we are doing. Right? Of course right.'

Amber reached out and hugged each of the girls tight and then slid off the bed and jumped to her feet.

'Dresses! We need dresses. Shoes. Hair. Bijou. Let's go and show the world what we can achieve once we set our minds to it! Ready? Let's do this!'

As it was, Saskia was still zipping Kate into her dress when there was a sharp knock on the door and Rick stuck his head inside the bedroom, with his hand covering his eyes, and totally ignored the screams and shouts to go away.

'Hey, gorgeous ladies. Thought you ought to know that Heath and Sam are waiting downstairs in the library and there is a small blonde in a huge hat standing in the hallway demanding champagne. Shall I escort her up?'

'Mum!' Amber squealed and grabbed Saskia's hand in terror.

Saskia patted her on the hand. 'Nothing to worry about. Richard Burgess—your mission is to chat to the mother of the bride. She will be excited and nervous and is bound to have spotted Amber's dad and his other family by now and be spitting tacks. Can you spare some of that charm of yours?'

Rick widened the gap between his fingers and gave a low growl of appreciation at Saskia in her dress, winked once and then closed the door.

'Was Rick wearing a kilt? Oh my,' Kate gulped.

'I know. And just for me. Imagine that.'

* * *

Ten minutes later, and a whole thirty seconds ahead of schedule on her planner, Saskia adjusted the position of her bridesmaid posy and followed the direction of the gasps of awe and delight. Amber was standing at the top of the curved white marble staircase, holding hands with her father—her real father, a tall elegant man who had arrived from Paris with his entire entourage the previous day. They were chatting and laughing gently and it was wonderful to see.

Then Amber lifted her head and smiled at Saskia and gave her the gentlest of nods. She was ready.

This was it. This was her moment. And Amber had never looked more beautiful. She knew that she was loved and it shone out like a beacon.

Amber the fashion model. Amber the concert pianist. And now Amber the bride.

Saskia turned and gave the signal to Parvita and the string quartet of award-winning musicians who she'd pulled from all around the world on New Year's Day for the performance of a lifetime.

On the first beat of the music, Amber took her father's arm and he kissed her on the cheek one last time, before turning and taking the first step, and then the next, down the curving stately staircase.

Kate had created a long slender column of stunning hand-worked lace over flowing layers of silk which showed Amber's figure and tanned complexion to perfection. All topped by an antique lace veil and diamond tiara that her parents had provided as their wedding present.

Amber was the loveliest bride that Saskia had ever seen. As she turned slightly to pass down the aisle formed by chairs covered in rich red and gold sari fabric, she looked back at Saskia over one shoulder and mouthed the words "thank you".

Amber had caught her first glimpse of Sam. Who was waiting to claim her as his own.

And it melted Saskia's heart all over again.

Kate stepped in just behind the small train on Amber's dress, and then it was her turn to walk down the aisle behind her two best friends. There was Heath, grinning at Kate with such love. Rick sat next to him. In a kilt! And when she drew closer he flashed her a lusty look that almost made her drop her posy!

They were three girls in love with three remarkable men who loved them back.

The snow had stopped falling and beams of brilliant sunshine broke through the clouds, creating a carpet of sparkling silver crystals on the snow-covered pergola and conifers on the other side of the glass.

It was fairy tale perfect. Magical.

Red flower petals gathered by the girls at the orphanage in India were strewn on the path leading to the lover's bower.

And as Amber's father lifted his daughter's hand and gave it to Sam, the musicians and singers burst out in an almighty *Halleluiah* that made the roof of the conservatory ring with the energy of it. And she could not be happier.

* * * * *

Mills & Boon® Hardback

October 2013

ROMANCE

MEDICAL

Mills & Boon® Large Print

October 2013

ROMANCE

The Sheikh's Prize	Lynne Graham
Forgiven but not Forgotten?	Abby Green
His Final Bargain	Melanie Milburne
A Throne for the Taking	Kate Walker
Diamond in the Desert	Susan Stephens
A Greek Escape	Elizabeth Power
Princess in the Iron Mask	Victoria Parker
The Man Behind the Pinstripes	Melissa McClone
Falling for the Rebel Falcon	Lucy Gordon
Too Close for Comfort	Heidi Rice
The First Crush Is the Deepest	Nina Harrington

HISTORICAL

Reforming the Viscount	Annie Burrows
A Reputation for Notoriety	Diane Gaston
The Substitute Countess	Lyn Stone
The Sword Dancer	Jeannie Lin
His Lady of Castlemora	Joanna Fulford

MEDICAL

NYC Angels: Unmasking Dr Serious	Laura Iding
NYC Angels: The Wallflower's Secret	Susan Carlisle
Cinderella of Harley Street	Anne Fraser
You, Me and a Family	Sue MacKay
Their Most Forbidden Fling	Melanie Milburne
The Last Doctor She Should Ever Date	Louisa George

0913 GEN STD LP

Mills & Boon® Hardback
November 2013

ROMANCE

MEDICAL

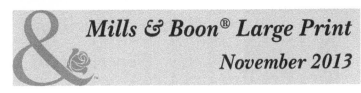

Mills & Boon® Large Print

November 2013

ROMANCE

HISTORICAL

MEDICAL